ROBERT B. PARKER

PLAYMATES

Thorndike Press • Thorndike, Maine

Also by Robert B. Parker
in Thorndike Large Print

• *The Widening Gyre*
• *A Savage Place*

Library of Congress Cataloging in Publication Data:

Parker, Robert B., 1932-
  Playmates / Robert B. Parker.
  p. cm.
  ISBN 0-89621-893-7 (alk. paper : lg. print)
  1. Large type books. I. Title.
[PS3566.A686P5   1989]   89-20218
813'.54--dc20   CIP

Thorndike Press Large Print edition published in 1989 by
arrangement with G. P. Putnam's Sons.

Cover design by Cynthia Bowen.

This book is printed on acid-free, high opacity paper. ∞

For Joan

ONE

Vince Haller invited me to lunch at the Clarendon Club on Commonwealth Avenue with the Chairman of the Board of Trustees of Taft University, Haller's alma mater.

"No sneakers," Haller told me. "No jeans, no open shirts with that idiotic gold chain you wear that's at least six years out of fashion."

"Susan gave it to me," I said.

"Sure," Haller said and gave me a look I'd seen him give witnesses during cross examination. It was a look that said *you are a bigger simp than Michael Jackson.*

Which is why, on the last day of February, I was strolling up Commonwealth in my gray suit wearing a blue oxford shirt with a traditional roll in the collar, and a yellow silk tie that whispered *power.* My cordovan loafers gleamed with polish, and I had a brand new Browning 9mm on my belt just back of my right hip. The Browning was flat and the

7

holster canted forward so that the gun snuggled into the hollow over my right kidney and didn't disturb the rakish drape of my suit. I was dressed to the nines, armed to the teeth, ready to lunch with the WASPs. If I hadn't been me, I'd have wished I were.

Haller was waiting for me in the entry hall. He was wearing a double breasted camel hair coat, and a winter vacation tan that seemed even darker around his gray hair and mustache. Haller said, "Spenser," in his big courtroom voice, and put out his hand. I took it. A retainer in a black suit took Haller's coat and hung it for him, and Haller and I went up the stairs toward the main dining room.

The Clarendon Club looked as it should. Twenty foot ceilings, curving marble staircase, dark oak paneling. It had once been the enclave of Bostonians of English descent, a redoubt outside of which the masses had huddled in appropriate exclusion. Now it was an ecumenical enclave, accepting anyone with money and pretending they were WASPs.

Baron Morton was waiting for us at a table. He stood when we approached. Haller introduced us and we shook hands and sat down.

"Drink to start, Mr. Spenser?" Morton said.

"Sure," I said.

A white-coated waiter was instantly there. I

8

ordered beer, Morton had Chivas-and-soda-tall-with-a-twist, Haller had a martini. The waiter scuttled off to get the drinks and I sat back to wait. I knew how this would go. Morton would fiddle around for a while, Haller would prompt him, and after a bit he'd tell me why we were having lunch.

"So you're a detective," Morton said. Haller's eyes were sweeping the room, picking out former clients and prospective clients; much of his work was criminal, but Vince was always alert.

"Yes," I said.

"How does one get into that line?"

"I was a cop and after a while I decided to go on my own," I said.

"Spenser had a little trouble conforming," Haller said. "He's, as I told you, Baron, a bit of a free spirit."

"Like a stormy kestrel," I said.

The waiter brought the drinks.

Morton took a dip into his and said, "Stormy kestrel, by God!" He laughed and shook his head. "What kind of living can someone make doing this, if I'm not being too nosy."

"Varies," I said. "Averages out to sufficient."

"Is there much danger?"

"Just enough," I said.

Morton smiled. The waiter handed out menus.

We ordered lunch.

"So what do you need from Spenser?" Haller said.

Morton looked apologetic. "I should be getting to the point, shouldn't I?"

I smiled politely.

"Just that I was so interested. I mean, you know, a private eye and all that."

I flattened my upper lip over my front teeth and said, "You ever stood out in the rain with your guts beat out?"

It sounded exactly like Humphrey Bogart. Morton looked at me blankly.

Haller said, "Spenser thinks he does impressions."

"Oh," Morton said. "Well, ah, I need some help on a fairly delicate matter."

The waiter brought our lunch. Chicken pot pie for Morton. Scrod for Haller. Red flannel hash for me. I drank some Sam Adams.

"You're familiar with Taft University?" Morton said.

"Yes."

"I'm the Chairman of the Board of Trustees, at Taft."

I put some ketchup on my hash.

"Do you follow college basketbal¹ Mr. Spenser?"

"Some. I like the pros better."

"Well, Taft, as perhaps you know, is a major basketball power. Not only in the east, but nationally."

"Made the final four, couple years ago," I said.

"Yes, and we're ranked in the top twenty again this year," Morton said.

"Kid, Dwayne Woodcock, is a piece of work," Haller said.

"Yes," Morton said. "Best power forward in the country."

"So what can I do for you," I said. "You looking for a point guard?"

Morton took in some air, slowly, and let it out slowly, through his nose.

"I guess I'll have to finally say it," he said.

I drank some Sam Adams and ate some hash.

"There's rumors of point shaving," Morton said.

"Ah," I said.

"The student newspaper first reported it, and a couple of sportswriters have said something about it to Brad Walker."

"Who's Walker?" I said.

"The A.D."

"How about the coach?"

"People don't like to give Dixie bad news. He reacts, ah, poorly to bad news," Morton said.

11

"Tends to kill the messenger," Haller said. He'd finished his scrod and was nearly through his second martini. It always puzzled me he could have that kind of lunch and then go into court and win cases.

"So no one's asked the coach," I said.

"No," Morton said.

"Anyone ask the players?"

"No. Dixie doesn't like people upsetting the players," Morton said.

"Does the college paper say where it got its rumor?"

Morton shook his head. "Kids say they're protecting their sources."

"How about the sportswriters?"

"Well, we haven't actually pressed this very far, Mr. Spenser. We didn't want to lend credence to the rumor, and we didn't want to encourage the rumors to circulate, if you see what I mean."

"So what is it you want me to do?"

"We want you to track the allegations down, establish their truth or falsity, put the matter to rest."

"What if they're true?" I said.

"If they are true we will turn the matter over to the district attorney. The university is not prepared to cover up illegal things," Morton said. "We care about our student athletes, and we care about a winning program at Taft.

But we also care about rule of law."

"I may have to annoy your coach," I said.

"I understand. He's a difficult, proud, volatile personality; but don't misjudge him. Dixie Dunham is a good man."

"We'll get along fine," I said.

Haller made a noise in his throat and then coughed into his clenched fist. Morton glanced at him and said nothing.

"If we can agree on the costs, are you willing to sign on for this?" Morton said.

"Sure," I said. "My fee increases twenty percent, though, if your coach is mean to me."

"Mr. Spenser," Morton said, "I can't promise . . ."

"He's kidding," Haller said. "He does that a lot."

"Oh, of course. Well, let's talk money."

We did. It wasn't hard, and when it was over I was employed again.

"Am I working for you, Mr. Morton, or the University?" I said.

"You are employed by the Board of Trustees and empowered to act on their behalf." He glanced at Haller for confirmation.

"Baron," Haller said. "It doesn't make any difference how you say it. He'll do what he wants to."

"Well, we will need a contract spelling out the parameters of the job, I think," Morton said.

"Sure," I said.

Haller made the sound in his throat again.

"I'll have the corporate counsel draft up something," Morton said.

"Fine," I said. "Are you the one I talk with when I need some access, or whatever?"

"If you'll come by the University, I'll introduce you to our President," Morton said. "He will be more effective in seeing that you get what you need."

The waiter came with the bill, and Morton discreetly signed it.

"Perhaps you could meet me at the President's office tomorrow," Morton said, "and we can talk about details and meet President Cort."

"What excitement," I said.

TWO

President Adrian Cort was a tall guy with a big Adam's apple and very energetic eyes. He told me I'd have full access to any information or facility I needed at the University, though he hoped I would find no need to be intrusive, and that the students and Coach Dunham both would be treated respectfully. I promised to do my best. He asked if I wanted someone to show me around the campus, and I said I'd rather wander on my own. Then we all said good bye. Morton and Cort called each other Baron and Adrian.

Alone at last, I strolled over toward the campus police station, walking extra softly in case Coach Dunham was in the area. From a cop at the desk I got a map of the campus, and took a one-hour stroll of orientation. Taft University occupies about forty acres west of Boston in a town called Walford. It had grown rapidly since the Second World War and the

15

core campus of ivy-covered brick buildings had been extensively augmented with a variety of architectural styles that blended like pieces from different puzzles. The dominant feel was of brutish slabs and confusion.

I found the Taft Daily Collegian in the Student Union Building on the second floor, looking out over the long narrow quadrangle that led to the angular glass and granite library. It was early afternoon. The thaw had departed and the hard sun was without warmth as it glinted on the snowy campus.

The newspaper office was busy. It looked like a small daily newspaper office, which it was, except that the staff was younger. A young woman wearing pink Reeboks directed me to the sports department in the far corner of the room, where three desks were pushed together to define a sort of horseshoe space underneath sports glossies stuck to the wall with map tacks. Most of the photographs had curled up around the single tack that held them. At one of the desks a young blond kid with a ragged crew cut was working on an Apple word processor. He wore jeans and a white shirt buttoned to the neck and he kept typing when I arrived at his desk. I consulted the list of names that President Cort had given me. Actually Cort hadn't given me the list. He'd spoken to his secretary and she had given it to me.

"Barry Ames?" I said.

The kid didn't look up. He kept typing, his eyes on the screen, but he paused long enough to raise his right hand for a moment and waggle it at me in a gesture that said, *wait*. He continued typing for maybe another full minute while I waited. Then he paused and looked up.

"Who was it you wanted?" he asked.

"Barry Ames," I said.

"That's me," he said. "Sorry to put you on hold like that, but when you're hot, you like to get it down before you lose it."

"Certainly," I said. "My name is Spenser, and the University has asked me to look into the question of point shaving by your basketball team."

"Are you a cop?"

"Private," I said.

"Holy shit, a private eye?"

"You wrote the column in which the allegation about point shaving was made, Barry?" It was the oldest of cop tricks. Use the guy's first name when you talk to him. He doesn't know yours, puts him slightly on the defensive.

"Why do you want to know?" Barry said.

"Because I want to know where you heard the rumor."

"That's privileged," Barry said.

"Barry, I'm too old to listen to horse shit. You made an allegation of criminal behavior based on hearsay. That in itself is irresponsible, maybe libelous."

"And maybe I want to talk to my lawyer," Barry said. Calling him by his first name had really softened him up.

"Let me put this another way," I said. "You printed a rumor that your team was shaving points. What did you expect would happen next?"

"That someone would investigate, for crissake," Barry was outraged.

"Right," I said.

Barry opened his mouth, and then paused, and then did a smart thing: he closed it.

I nodded encouragingly.

"Well, I still can't tell you my sources," Barry said.

"Is it a reliable source?" I said.

"It was a girl who dated one of the team guys."

"She should know," I said.

"She didn't say she knew. She just said she'd heard somebody sort of hint at it, you know, joking."

"Who was she dating?"

Barry shook his head. "I won't tell you. I'm not going to get her in trouble."

"Why would she get in trouble?" I said.

Barry shook his head some more.

"At the moment no one's talking about prosecuting on this thing, but if they do, and your rumor is correct, then you're going to get asked this question again under the threat of a contempt citation," I said. "Then it's grown up time, kid."

"You think I'm a kid and a kid doesn't know shit, don't you," Barry said.

"Exactly," I said.

A number of Barry's colleagues had gathered silently about during this interplay. None of them seemed to be rooting for me.

"Whyn't you get off his case, Mister," said a young woman with very large pink-rimmed glasses.

"You happen to know the source of his rumor?" I said.

"No, but if I did, I wouldn't tell you."

I looked at the rest of the kids, slowly, one at a time. Nobody said anything.

"What's too bad," I said, "is you've fastened on to the wrong principle. The heart of the business is not protecting your sources. It's spreading the truth."

None of them said anything except one in the back, who said, "Yeaa!" And another kid said, "It's Lou Grant."

Then a girl giggled and three or four others laughed. It is hard to remain dignified when being laughed at by a group of adolescents. I succeeded, however. I left without giving them the finger.

THREE

The "Taft Basketball Program" looks like *Life* magazine. It's in full color. It has biographies of all the players on both sides, pictures of everybody, individual statistics, and a history of the rivalry, which was Georgetown on a program Cort's secretary had given me. I had it rolled up and stuck in my left hip pocket when I drifted into the Taft field house and took a seat in the empty stands above the basketball court, put my feet up on the seats in front of me and spread out to watch the Taft Falcons practice. They were running switch drills in opposite corners of the floor under a couple of assistant coaches, and the head coach, Dixie Dunham, moved back and forth, commenting, correcting, reviling.

"Awright," Dunham was screaming. "Everybody around me down here." The group at the far left of the court came down to the far right end where Dunham was standing.

"Okay," Dunham said, "Dwayne, you got the ball. You pass off to Dennis, come down here, set the pick. Dennis, you go off and pick to the right. Now . . . okay, . . . Robert, what do you do?"

"Fight through the pick, Coach."

"And if you do, and Kenny thinks you're going to switch, what happens?"

There was silence for a moment.

"What the fuck happens?" Dunham's voice went up an octave.

"Both guys guarding Dennis," Dwayne said. "I roll to the basket."

"That's right. Come on, boys, is Dwayne the only one of you thinking? So what do you learn from that? What's the lesson we take. What does my system say about that?"

"We got to talk to each other," Robert said.

"Check," Dunham said, "and double check. That, Robert, is the sixty-four-thousand-dollar key. You got to talk. I don't care whether you switch, or you fight through the pick. Both of you got to know what the other guy's doing, otherwise, what? Kenny, what?"

"Two for them, Coach."

"You bet your ass." Dunham clapped his hands. "Okay, Frank, Billy, take them back, let's work on it some more."

Dunham was a legend. Certainly he was one of the two or three best college basketball coaches in the country. He was also a man of legendary temper and intensity and had sat out a five-game suspension a couple of years ago when he had gone into the stands after a heckler. Since he was six feet five and weighed maybe 225, when he went after the heckler it constituted a genuine threat. According to the program he'd been a small forward at Canisius, had averaged eight points, three assists and four rebounds a game, in a college career during which Canisius had won seventy and lost eighteen. He'd coached at Seton Hall, and then at Marquette, before he'd come to Taft, and he'd always won.

I sat quietly in the stands, one of maybe five or six people watching practice, and learning the players by comparing their pictures on last week's program with the faces on the court. In maybe twenty-five minutes I had them all memorized and attached to names.

I watched them scrimmage. I watched Dunham go into a frenzy at one point and send them all to the locker room, only to bring them back out of the locker room two minutes after they'd gone in. Finally the practice wound down and the players were shooting free throws at several baskets around the court.

Dunham turned away from this and looked up at me in the stands. Then he walked straight up the stairs from the court and over to me.

"What the fuck are you doing?" he said.

"What a clever way to ask," I said.

"I want to know what you're doing here," he said. "You're not a student."

"Now you don't know that," I said. "I might have stayed back a lot."

"Look, I'm not here to bullshit with you. You give me straight answers or I'll have your ass thrown out of this gym."

"Okay," I said. "I'm a spy from Syracuse. I've learned your secret, talk to each other on the switches."

"Listen to me, buster. And listen good," Dunham said. "I spotted you with the program half an hour ago. Why are you studying my players?"

I was laughing. " 'Listen to me, buster, and listen good'?" I said. "For crissake, Dixie."

Dunham glared at me for five seconds and then his face began to crease into a slowly widening grin.

"Shit," he said. "I talk that way all the time."

I shook my head.

Dunham said, "I still want to know what you're doing here." His face was mixed laughter and anger. "And I can still by God kick your ass if I have to."

I was still laughing, though it had calmed

some and I kept it inside where it only made a murmur in my chest.

"Not if you fight like you talk," I said.

It is hard to be a tough guy when the intended victim is laughing at you. Dixie wasn't used to being laughed at. He wasn't quite sure what to do. The fact that he was half laughing too tended to compromise his position.

"Look," I said, and then I couldn't resist it, "and look good," I said. And this time Dunham laughed, before I did. I tried again. "Dixie," I said, "what I'm doing here takes some explanation. If you'll stop yelling at me and sit down and listen you'll learn a lot."

Dixie stared at me for a bit and then said, "I got to get these kids showered and out of here. I'll meet you for a drink in an hour."

"Okay."

"Local place, the Lancaster Tap," Dunham said. "On College Ave."

"Saw it when I drove in today," I said.

Dunham looked at his watch. "Be there about six," he said, and turned away and marched down to the court and across it and into the corridor on the far side. The team ended practice the minute he entered the corridor and trailed in behind him. A couple of undergraduates, one of them female, began picking up the basketballs. It had been a long time since I played. But I could remember the feel of the ball, the control as you bounced it, your hand knowing the ball would come back and when and where, bouncing it again in control, pulling up, the ball resting mostly on the fingers, the shot, the arc, just as your hand had specified. *Swish* . . . Well, sometimes swish. Often, *Clang*.

FOUR

Dixie was glaring at me again, across a scarred table in a booth at the Lancaster Tap. I had a draft beer, Dixie had a large Coke. Between us were menus. On the table top in front of me was carved RP + JH. The table top was covered with initials, but RP + JH was carved deeper, and looked more permanent.

Dixie was holding the large Coke in his right hand. He leveled his right forefinger at me.

"I'm here to tell you that's bullshit," Dixie said. "Not one of those boys would do that to me. Not one ever has and not one ever will."

I nodded. On the walnut paneled walls of the pub were pictures of Taft teams and players. There was a prominent picture of Dixie with the National Championship team.

"University rules for eligibility are a two point oh average. Mine is two point three. Every player graduates with his class. Every one. Kids know that once they've been in this

27

program, they're part of this program for the rest of their lives. You unnerstand that? Whenever the Trail Blazers are in town, Troy Murphy comes over, helps out at practice, sits on the bench during a game. Still calls me Coach. When the Pistons cut Stevie Scott, who'd he call? I got him an assistant's job with Rollie at Villanova, one phone call."

A little of Dixie's Coke slopped over the edge of his glass. He put the glass down, wiped his hand with a napkin.

"This isn't a bunch of free-lance schoolyard assholes, Jack," Dixie said. "This is a team. This is a system. Greatest system ever devised to play this game. No way, you hear me? No way anybody is going to betray that system, no fucking way they're going to turn their backs on their team. No way any of those boys would turn his back on me."

Dixie had his intimidate-the-referee glare locked on me. I said, "I guess you don't think they're shaving points, Dixie."

"You are out of line, Buddy Boy." Dixie turned up the voltage on his stare. "And if I hear that kind of talk out of you or anyone else you're going to answer to me. You unnerstand me?"

I drank a little beer, wiped my mouth politely with the back of my hand, and smiled pleasantly.

"Dixie," I said, "establishing the truth of this point shaving stuff will require that I keep running in to you for a while. It's going to be a lot easier if we clear up something now. You're a big strong guy, and you're probably in shape. But I've been doing this most of my life and if we have a fight I will put you in the hospital."

Dixie stared at me without speaking, which was a relief. The Lancaster Tap was only half full. There were faculty-looking people having an early dinner, and a few parents with children dining out family style. It was the kind of place that would fill up later as the college kids came in to drink. There was only one booth full so far, at the opposite corner of the room. Drinking tequila with a Corona chaser, the kids were relatively subdued. As their ranks swelled I assumed they'd get noisier.

Dixie said, "How many times your nose been broken?"

"Several," I said.

The waitress came over to our table. She looked like Knute Rockne.

"You want to order, Coach?"

Dixie shook his head. "Not yet, Lila."

"That scar tissue around your eyes?" Dixie said.

I nodded.

29

"You used to fight."

I nodded.

"Any good?"

I nodded.

"Ever fight anybody I ever heard of?"

"Joe Walcott, once," I said. "In the Garden. He was way past it, and I was just coming along. They threw me in to give Joe an easy one."

"And?"

"It's one of the times my nose got busted."

"Did he have an easy fight?"

"Easier than I did," I said.

"How much you weigh when you were fighting?" Dixie said.

"Hundred ninety-two."

"How much you weigh now?"

"Two oh one."

"Stayed in shape," Dixie said.

"Yeah."

"I fight it all the time. I'm down to two twenty-five now, but it's a struggle."

I nodded. Dixie picked up his menu and began to study it. I looked at mine.

"Mixed grill's good here," Dixie said.

I nodded. The waitress returned and took out her order book.

"Mixed grill, Coach?" she said.

"You bet, Lila, and another Coke."

She wrote it down eagerly and looked at me

like I shouldn't dawdle. I ordered a club sandwich.

Lila lumbered off with the orders.

"You think I didn't see the column in the *Collegian?* Dumb ass kid writes it, what's his name?"

"Barry Ames," I said.

"Yeah, *Ames' Games* he calls it. Thinks he's Roger Angell."

"Most people aren't."

"This jerk isn't," Dixie said.

"So you knew there was talk of point shaving," I said. "You talk to the players?"

"I told them, 'Boys, anyone says that to you, you let me know, and I'll nail his ass up on the door of my office.'"

"You didn't ask them if it was so?"

"I tole you," Dixie said. "It ain't so."

"Dixie," I said, "somebody's got to ask them."

Dixie tilted his head back and let the ice cubes drain from his glass into his mouth. He crunched them with his teeth and rolled the fragments around in his mouth for a minute and then talked around the ice.

"We beat Syracuse Monday and we take the Conference championship. The playoffs come up in another week. Our first eight are as good as anybody's and we got one legitimate all-American. We don't get hurt and we could go the whole way. We don't have the stud in the middle, but Dwayne offsets that considerably."

Lila came back and slapped a green salad down in front of Dixie. It was sloshed with orange-colored dressing. Dixie swallowed his ice.

"You mind?" he said.

I shook my head and Dixie began to eat the salad. He acted like it was good.

"You figure that a point shaving investigation, even if it turns out to be groundless, will screw these kids' heads up," I said.

Dixie put his fork down and looked up from his salad.

"You know goddamned well it will," he said.

"I don't suppose they could shave points without you knowing it," I said.

Dixie snorted. Lila came with his mixed grill. There was a lamb chop, a kidney, a sausage, two strips of bacon, and a small minute steak. On the side was a large mound of french fries and a saucer of cubed carrots. Dixie sprinkled half a cellar of pepper on the carrots. Lila put my club sandwich in front of me. Her body language suggested that she found me unworthy to eat with the coach.

"Nobody's saying they're losing games, Dixie. Just beating the spread."

"You stay away from those boys, Spenser. You stay out of my gym, you stay away from my kids. Not one of them will talk to you."

"Because you told them not to."

"Because I told them not to. We've worked too hard to have you screw up our season now with some harebrained dip shit investigation so you can make a few bucks off the University."

"I can't do it, Dixie."

Dixie was silent for a while. The room was filling up. All the spots at the bar were full and most of the booths. The people at the bar were mostly Walford townies. The booths were full of college kids.

"Spenser, I swing a lot of weight aroun here," Dixie said. "You keep pressing th thing and I'll use some of it."

"Okay if I finish my sandwich," I said.

That was as far as I got with Dixie D ham. I finished my club sandwich. He ished his mixed grill. He paid and when left in silence I knew nothing I hadn't kn when I came in. Maybe a little less.

FIVE

"Why not talk with the best player," Susan said. We were in my kitchen, Susan sipping coffee at my counter while I was attempting johnny cake for the third time, trying to get the batter thick enough to form cakes on the griddle.

"Because the coach can intimidate him less?"

"Maybe. Have they got a best player?"

"Dwayne Woodcock," I said.

"If he disobeys the coach what would be the punishment?"

"He doesn't play."

"And if he doesn't play does the team go down the tubes, or whatever revolting sports cliché fits?"

"The team suffers," I said. "Don't shrinks use clichés?"

"It would not be appropriate," Susan said and smiled at me as Mephistopheles might

34

have smiled at Faust.

"Worth a try," I said. The johnny cake had been on the griddle nearly ten minutes and was holding its shape, although it had spread out to be a bigger cake than I had in mind. I edged the spatula under it and when it was loose I flipped it carefully. The shape held.

"What are those doughballs you're cooking?" Susan said.

I shook my head sadly. "You Jewesses know nothing about honest down-home cooking," I said. "This is johnny cake, rich in history and tradition, favored by goyim in this part of the country for three hundred years."

Susan shrugged. "Vot do day know from fency cooking?" she said.

"I seem to remember that punch line in slightly different form," I said.

"I destroyed the alliteration," she said.

I pressed down on the johnny cake with the spatula. It did not sizzle. I slid it onto a plate and put it on the counter in front of Susan. I spread on a bit of butter and splashed on some dark amber Vermont maple syrup. I cut a piece for her and held it out.

"Take a bite," I said. "Learn something."

She nibbled it off the fork with a bright flash of teeth and chewed thoughtfully.

"Fried mush?" she said.

"Well, maybe a distant cousin," I said. "It's

white cornmeal, mostly. Originated with the Indians."

"Can I have some lox with it," Susan said.

Susan managed to eat three johnny cakes, without lox, and I put away four, and two cups of coffee. Susan was wearing the white silk peignoir I braved Victoria's Secret to buy her for Christmas. She had no makeup on and I could tell what she'd looked like when she was a little girl. Except when she looked at me. The eyes were not those of a little girl. The eyes had seen life intimately and clearly.

"Gee," I said, "that robe seems to fall open very revealingly."

"Must be a design flaw," Susan said.

"Well, I certainly wouldn't have bought it if I'd known it was a second," I said.

"The thought of you in Victoria's Secret is heart warming, though," Susan said.

"I blushed," I said.

"Good to know you can," Susan said and got up and started putting on her makeup. I cleaned up breakfast and went to shower and shave.

Two hours later, with the johnny cake still sticking to my ribs, I fell into step across the Taft Quadrangle with Dwayne Woodcock. At six feet nine and 255 pounds Dwayne was the premier power forward in the country; he was also probably the number one pick in the

NBA draft next year, and, according to the papers, a fair head case. Most men his size played center in college and switched to forward in the pros. The Taft center in fact was six foot seven, but Dwayne had made that condition when he came to Taft. He would be the power forward, giving him a four-year start on his pro position. Walking beside him was walking in the shade.

"Dwayne Woodcock?" I said.

He looked down at me silently and, after a moment, nodded.

"My name is Spenser. I need to talk with you for a moment."

"Know who you are, man."

"You on your way to class?"

Woodcock smiled and shook his head. "Breakfast."

"Good, mind if I join you?"

"Coach says I ain't supposed to talk with you," Dwayne said. There was no apology in his voice, or embarrassment. He was just reporting a fact to me.

"You always do what Coach says?"

"Don't do what nobody says, man. Do what Dwayne Woodcock says." Again the smile, genuine, but not friendly, condescending, as if to say he would overlook the fact that I was a short old white guy. It was probably hard not to seem condescending if you were

Dwayne's size. You looked down from above the everyday world.

"So what does Dwayne Woodcock say about having breakfast with me?" I said.

"Free country, man, you want to walk along, okay with me."

As we walked across the campus a hundred people said hello to Dwayne. He was friendly but regal.

"So what you want to talk about, man?"

"Didn't Coach tell you?"

Dwayne smiled again. "Naw. Coach don't do a lot of telling. He just say stay the fuck away from you and not to talk with you."

"What happens if you do talk with me?"

"Me? Nothing."

"How about somebody else?" I said.

" 'My way or highway,' Coach always say."

"How come nothing happens to you?"

"Man, don't you know nothing? Coach wants that final four so bad, he eat shit to get there. I don't play, he don't get it."

"Well, I'm a detective and the University has hired me to see if there's any truth to the rumors of point shaving."

Dwayne frowned down at me.

"You what?" he said. And I realized I'd gone too fast for him.

"I'm a private detective," I said. I'd feed it to him in small bits.

"Like fucking Magnum, PI?"

"Just like him, except I do it in Boston."

"What kind of wheels you got, man?"

"I'm driving a Jeep for the winter," I said. "Love that four by four." I also drove it in the spring and summer and fall and would drive it for a number of seasons to come.

"You carrying, man?"

"Sure." I opened my coat to let him see the Browning. "The University hired me."

"The University," Dwayne said. "This place? You working for this place?"

"Un huh. They heard that there was point shaving going on."

"Point shaving? They hired you to investigate fucking point shaving?"

"Yeah. Article awhile ago in the college paper about it. You see it?"

Dwayne shook his head. "No, man. I never read that shit."

We reached one of the campus dining rooms and went in. It was in a lovely Georgian brick building with a big, small-paned picture window that looked out onto the quadrangle. Inside was mostly white walls and quarry tile. Dwayne had four fried eggs, over easy, two orders of bacon, home fries, four pieces of white toast, two large orange juices, and two containers of milk. I had coffee. Regular, two sugars. I would have had decaf but I didn't want Dwayne to think I was a sissy. The dining room was nearly full, but Dwayne led me to a section marked Faculty Only where there were plenty of seats. We sat at a table for four and Dwayne spread his food out over most of it.

"So, man, what you want to talk about?"

"There's a rumor that some of the players on the Taft basketball team are getting paid off for shaving points," I said. "Can you tell me anything about that?"

"How come you talking to me, man?"

"Because I know that Dixie told his players not to talk with me and I figured maybe you'd be the only one with balls enough to do it anyway."

"Dwayne Woodcock talk to whoever he fucking wants," Dwayne said.

"What I figured," I said. "So what do you think?"

"Nobody throwing no games, man," Dwayne said.

"I know. But are they keeping the score down so that someone can beat the point spread?"

Dwayne shook his head. "No chance, man."

"Would you know it if they were?"

"Shit, man, I know everything going on out there. Dwayne Woodcock born playing this game, you know? Who say we dogging it?"

"Just a rumor, printed in the college paper."

"Who start the rumor?"

"Some guy was kidding about it in front of his girlfriend, or so they say at the paper."

"School paper?"

"Yeah, the *Taft Collegian.*"

"Shit, they don't matter."

I shrugged.

"Who the girlfriend?" Dwayne said.

"They didn't know."

"Who you talk to over that newspaper?"

"Kid named Barry Ames." Dwayne could find out easily enough. I might as well earn points by telling him. I liked his interest.

Dwayne shook his head. "Never heard of him."

We were quiet for a moment while I drank a little coffee and Dwayne ate.

"So, maybe you wasting your time here. Broad probably didn't understand what the guy was joking about. Probably some kind of basketball joke and she don't get it."

"Maybe," I said.

"You keep hanging around, man, annoying us, everybody gonna get pissed off at you."

I nodded. "Happens a lot," I said.

"You understand what I'm saying to you, man? Dwayne Woodcock don't blow smoke."

"That's not what Smoke tells everybody," I said.

Dwayne gave me the hard schoolyard stare. "You fucking with me, man?"

"Yeah."

"You fucking with Dwayne Woodcock, you fucking with the wrong man."

"Who would be the right one?" I said.

Dwayne had no food left. He surveyed the table to make sure he hadn't missed anything. Then he stood up. Looking down at me, he said, "You remember what I tell you, man. You keep snooping around, you going to wish you hadn't." Then he turned and stalked off.

I gave his back a grim look as he went.

"Oh yeah," I said.

SIX

In the spirit of experiment I checked out the coeds as I walked across campus and concluded that I was still able to respond to twenty-year-old women, but preferred them older. At the President's office I consulted with Ms. Merriman, the President's secretary. She, for instance, was older.

"I need a copy of Dwayne Woodcock's transcript, academic record, whatever; any documentation on him that the University has."

Ms. Merriman frowned.

"It's not policy to show material like that without the student's authorization."

Ms. Merriman was very trim and well dressed. She was maybe forty-five with a tight body and short black very curly hair. She wore an engagement ring on the wrong hand and no wedding ring. Her dark blue tailored suit must have set her back about $600. She treated me like some sort of distinguished barbarian, like the king of a very important cannibal nation who still wore a bone in his nose.

"We'll find a way," I said.

"You feel it's necessary?"

"I have no idea," I said. "Detective stuff doesn't really lend itself to 'policy' decisions. Detective stuff is pretty much weaseling around and finding out anything you can and then sitting down afterward and figuring out what's worth knowing."

"I don't know. I don't feel right about it."

"Why don't you consult with President Cort."

Her eyes widened. "Well, he's in an important meeting right now . . ."

"Something crucial?" I said. "Like whether full professors should be required to show up at all?"

"Mr. Spenser, please."

"Or whether a book that sells can be considered favorably in the course of a tenure decision."

"Mr. Spenser. Running a large university like this one is a serious administrative challenge. President Cort's time is as important as any executive's."

"I rest my case," I said. "But let's not argue. Let's compromise. Call up somebody and get me Dwayne's file."

"President Cort did say you should have our full support."

I nodded encouragement.

"All right, these are unusual circumstances. I'll call the registrar's office."

"God," I said, "you're beautiful when you're decisive."

"Oh, please," she said. But she went to the phone and called. In about fifteen minutes an undergraduate-looking kid showed up with a manila envelope and handed it to Ms. Merriman. She opened it, saw that it was what she'd ordered, closed it again and handed it to me.

"I hope you'll return that straight here once you are through with it."

"Right here," I said. I gave her the complete smile. The one where my eyes crinkle at the corners and two deep dimples appear in my cheeks. Women often tore off their underwear and threw it at me when I gave them the complete smile.

Ms. Merriman didn't.

I left the office and found the library and settled into a yellow oak chair with arms, near a window in the reading room.

According to the transcript of his grades Dwayne was a B − , C + student. He was on full scholarship, had been before the Dean for two incidents of fighting and a charge of larceny. The charge, apparently brought by another student, was dropped. There were several evaluations of Dwayne from his academic counselor, a woman named Madelaine Roth, Ph.D. The evaluations all stressed Dwayne's native intelligence despite his impoverished background. According to the transcript Dwayne had grown up in the Bedford-Stuyvesant section of Brooklyn, had a mother and four sisters, all on welfare. No father.

I settled back a little deeper in the chair and put my feet up on the window ledge and watched the students move across the campus. Most of them were noisy and oddly dressed and looked hung over. A few were carefully dressed, some of the girls wore eye shadow, many of the girls wore very tight jeans. I rolled my head a little on my neck to loosen my shoulders. The sun coming through the windows fell warmly on my back.

Dwayne had seemed too easy to talk to. He'd seemed too interested in who knew what. Or maybe I just thought so because I wanted to. Because it would be a place to start. Either way the transcript didn't tell me much. I swung my feet off the window sill and stood and brought the transcript back to Ms. Merriman.

SEVEN

Lennie Seltzer still had the back booth in the Yorktown Tavern on Mass. Ave. He was normally there from ten in the morning till four in the afternoon, sipping beer, reading newspapers, taking bets, getting up to use the pay phone on the back wall next to the rest rooms. His hair was shiny slick and parted in the middle. His face was pale and smooth. His three-piece suit had a fine windowpane plaid in pale blue running through the gray sharkskin fabric. He was getting plumper as time passed and a lot of the plumpness settled as he sat each day sipping beer. On the table in front of him were the *New York Daily News*, the *Globe* and the *Herald*. To his right, on the table against the wall, a portable computer screen stared grayly at me.

Lennie was tipping his beer glass delicately toward his lips when I slid into the booth opposite him. He held the glass with his thumb and first two fingers. His ring finger and pinkie were extended. He drank only a little of the beer and set the glass back down.

"Spenser," he said and made a gesture to the bartender.

"Lennie, you've moved into the age of tomorrow," I said.

The bartender brought over a shot of whiskey and a draft beer in a tall thick glass. I hated a shot of whiskey, but every time I saw Lennie he ordered it for me. Over the years the shot had upgraded. Now it was Irish whiskey, at least. When I first knew him it was Old Thompson.

"Computer's a wonderful thing, buddy. Got all my files in there, plug it into a phone jack, dial up everything I need. I have to close quickly, I just unplug it, fold it up and off I go."

"You think it's immoral, Lennie, to take a nap during the day?"

Lennie shook his head. "Hell, no. I take one every afternoon. I get home about four thirty, lie down for an hour, on my back, peaceful, get up, take a shower, couple a high-balls, sets you up for the night, you know? Take the old lady to Jimmy's, maybe, Doyle's in JP, fish dinner, bottle a wine. The nap's the key to it."

"I need to know the line on every Taft basketball game this year," I said. "And the final score."

Lennie looked at me for a little longer than was comfortable.

"You think somebody's been dicking with the spread over there?"

"I don't know. I'm trying to find out."

"You know something you got to tell me," Lennie said. "It's business, you know. I mean if something's not kosher I could get flushed on one of those games."

"I know. All I got now is rumors. Everybody connected with the team denies it. I come up with anything, I'll tell you. In confidence."

"Confidence is part of being a bookie, buddy, you know that. I don't talk about anything I don't need to."

"Can you get me the line?" I said. "I can get the scores from the newspaper file at the library if I have to."

"You come to the right place," Lennie said. "I can get you both in about ten minutes." He tapped the gray screen. "I used to have it all on slips of paper."

"Hard to flush that thing down the toilet," I said.

"No need. Unplug it and there's nothing on me. No evidence unless they search my home and access the computer." Lennie grinned.

"Besides, cops don't try too hard with me."

He turned on the machine and punched in a few codes. The screen turned black and printing came up on it in star wars green. Lennie gazed at it for a moment, took another delicate sip of beer, put the glass down carefully and punched some new keys.

Lennie reached under the table and came up with a slim, tan briefcase. He opened it, took out a yellow legal-sized pad, selected a pen from among the several that were clipped to one of the pockets. He put the pen on the table top beside the pad, closed the briefcase, put it back under the table and punched some more keys. This time he copied down the information on display, punched some more, wrote some more. After about fifteen minutes, Lennie had a couple of columns of dates and numbers on his pad. He put the cap on his pen, put it down, punched away the display, turned off the terminal, and the computer screen went gray.

"Okay," Lennie said. "This column the date of the game. This column the point spread. This column the score."

A bartender came over with a fresh glass of beer for Lennie and took away the empty glass. Lennie took the cap off his pen and ran down the columns of numbers like an accountant scanning a tax form.

"Here," he said, and put a check mark next to one of the dates. "And here," he said, "and here." When he was through there were six games checked.

"Here's the games where they beat the spread," Lennie said. "Could happen, and be legit. Basketball's hard to handicap."

"I know," I said. "The Nets beat the Celtics at the Garden this year."

Lennie nodded vigorously. "Exactly," he said.

I finished off my whiskey and stared at the beer. My head was beginning to feel thick and my face felt a little separate from the world, as if there were a transparent layer of insulation on it. Be a nice title for a novel, I thought, *Boilermakers in the Afternoon*. I took the sheet of yellow paper and folded it and put it into my shirt pocket.

"You still with that Jewish broad?" Lennie said.

"Susan," I said. "Susan Silverman."

"You gonna get married?"

"You never know," I said.

"You marry a Jew, and you and me be like lunsmen."

"Oy vay," I said.

EIGHT

I had to promise Ms. Merriman the right of first refusal on my sex life, but I managed to get her to call the athletic director on my behalf and tell him that the President wanted me to have tapes of six Taft basketball games. The A.D. told her that Dixie would have a fit if he found out, and Ms. Merriman said that Coach Dunham worked for the University and not the other way around and should he hear of it and complain he should be directed to her.

"What if Dixie calls you up and yells at you," I said.

"We are not here to service the basketball team," Ms. Merriman said.

"Good to know," I said.

"Yes," Ms. Merriman said.

By early afternoon I was lying on Susan's bed in her place watching the tape of late January's game between Taft and Seton Hall, on her VCR. Taft had been favored by seven and had won by three. I tried to watch away from the ball, at who was blocking out, who was rebounding, who was tight up on his man in the pressure man-to-man that Dixie insisted on in the age of zone. It's hard to watch basketball that way, even if you've played, even if you know the game. We are conditioned by television so to watch the ball. We tend not to notice weak side help, and who doubles down in the middle.

I watched the game through once without seeing anything that got my attention. This was going to take awhile. I watched the game through again, focusing for a while on one player, then another. The films were scouting films, not television, so they showed more of the court and spent less time fixed on the ball, and they didn't cover the time outs or half time, so the films only took a little more than an hour to watch. By three in the afternoon I'd watched Seton Hall twice and had concluded that I needed help. Also lunch.

For help I called a guy I knew named Tommy Christopher. He'd played at DePaul and then with the Celtics and had coached for six years at Providence College. When he was playing he'd had a good business manager and now Tommy mostly played golf, and a little poker, did a few commercials, and worked out at the Harbor Health Club, where he and I and Hawk now and then did some steam together.

I called the Harbor Health Club and left a message for Tommy to call me at Susan's.

"What's going on?" Henry said. "An afternooner?"

"More deadly than the adder's sting," I said, "is the foul mouth of an unusually short gym owner."

"I'm not unusually short," Henry said. "I'm just muscular for my height."

"Hell, yes," I said. "If you weighed twenty pounds you'd be just right."

We hung up and I looked into lunch. Susan seemed to me the most beautiful and intelligent woman I'd ever met. She had great warmth and compassion and humor. She had a top-of-the-line body, and strength of character and an appropriate sexual appetite. But as a larder keeper she ranked somewhat below Old Mother Hubbard. In her refrigerator was a plastic bag of raw cauliflower, a half empty carton of Dannon tropical fruit yogurt, a single round of whole wheat Syrian bread, which was unwrapped and had begun to fossilize, a jar of mayonnaise and a lemon. In her cupboard was a package of Rye Wafers, a jar of instant decaf, a loaf of whole wheat bread and, shamefully, a jar of all-natural peanut butter.

"Ah ha," I said. I boiled some water, made two peanut butter sandwiches, poured the hot water over a spoonful of decaf crystals, stirred twice, put the spoon in the sink and settled down at Susan's counter. Bon appétit.

While I was enjoying my second sandwich, Tommy Christopher called.

"Henry says you want to see me," Tommy said. "Said you needed help. I said you needed more help than I could give you."

"Susan's working on that," I said. "I need you to watch some basketball with me."

I explained what I had and what I wanted and Tommy said he'd come over.

"How many games are we going to watch?" Tommy said.

"Six," I said.

"I'll bring some beer," Tommy said.

Susan got through with her last patient at six and came upstairs from her office to find Tommy and me sprawled on her bed staring at the tapes. I had a notebook and wrote down what Tommy said.

"See that," Tommy was saying, "run it again. See Woodcock, he olés the forward on the weak side, and the guy comes in and takes the rebound and jams it."

"This is what you do all day?" Susan said. "I thought you were out fighting crime."

I hit the pause button. "Things are not what they seem," I said.

"I've heard that," Susan said.

NINE

We stopped watching after another hour that night and ate Chinese food that Susan had called out for and I had fetched. Then Tommy went home, and I stayed. Two nights in a row. Zowie.

Friday Tommy came in at nine and we settled in on the bed again and watched Taft against Pittsburgh.

"There," Tommy said. "Tubbs didn't fill the lane on the break, see on the left. So Davis takes it to the basket and draws the defender and has no place to lay it off and gets stuffed. He shouldn't have gone up in the air until he knew he had something to do with the ball, but it's reasonable to expect somebody to be filling that left hand lane. Then they'd have had a three on two." I scribbled in my notebook.

"Woodcock again," Tommy said. "You can see that play's set up for a pick. Stop, run it back. See the guard with the ball. He's yelling out a play. Okay, see, he comes out of the corner, loops around the perimeter, looking for the pick, and Woodcock is slow setting it. So Davis's got to back off and set up something else, and, see, they don't make the forty-five-second clock."

Benefiting from yesterday's learning experience, I had laid in a supply of smoked turkey sandwiches from the Mt. Auburn Market, and at noon we broke for a couple of them, each, with Cape Cod potato chips and Sam Adams beer; and back to the tapes.

"See, there's the same play that Woodcock fucked up this morning against Pittsburgh," Tommy said. "Look at this pick. Jesus Christ!"

I was sitting up on the edge of the bed so I wouldn't nod off.

"Okay, now here's another one. Run this back about ten seconds. Okay, there. Okay. It's Woodcock again. Simple give and go. The guard, what's his name, Davis, is going to find Woodcock in the corner, and then, the simplest play in basketball, he cuts for the basket. See. He loses his man. Amazing how often it works. He's free, the Temple center is too far toward Woodcock. And Woodcock holds the ball."

"Did he see him?"

"Spenser," Tommy said. "They've run that give and go twenty times in these tapes. They've run it twenty thousand times in their lives. Guy in the corner knows, *knows* there's going to be a cutter."

I turned it back and ran it again.

"See," Tommy said. "The minute he gets the ball, he dips his shoulders like he's going to drive. He never looks for the cutter, even though he's double teamed, and Taft has to pull it out and start over."

"Wouldn't any coaching staff see this reviewing the films?"

"If they were looking for it. And, face it, if you're coaching Taft, you're not looking for Dwayne Woodcock as a key to your loss, you know. He's probably the best player in the country."

"But if you did notice it," I said.

"You write it off as 'Dwayne's a known head case anyway.' Passing off is not the strongest part of his game."

"And," I said, "unless you see it as part of a pattern, and you were looking for the pattern, it wouldn't seem like anything but a break in concentration."

Tommy nodded. The tapes rolled on.

At four fifteen in the afternoon we finished the last tape.

"I say it's Woodcock," Tommy said. "And

he's smart about it. He's not missing lay ups and foul shots. He's just slowing down their game, keeps the score a few baskets lower. And he's so good that if they are in danger of losing because of that he can explode for five hoops in a row. I mean there isn't anyone in college ball that can stop him when he makes up his mind to drive."

"What he's doing is keeping his teammates from scoring as much," I said.

Tommy nodded approvingly. "Exactly," he said. "That's exactly what he does. Misses a pass, sets a sloppy pick, doesn't roll to the basket, doesn't block out underneath, is a step slow filling the lane. Usually the result is that another guy doesn't score."

"And," I said, "since they're winning most of these games, no one is questioning the outcome. Anyone else?"

"Maybe number eleven, what's his name."

"Davis," I said.

"There's nothing here I can swear to," Tommy said. "Can't take shit like this into court, but Woodcock, for sure. Maybe the other kid."

Tommy and I had one more beer and talked about the kinds of picks Wayne Embry used to set, and Wes Unseld. Then he went home and I packed the tapes back to the A.D.'s office at Taft.

It had gotten dark as I drove home. The commuter traffic was headed the other way. Susan was having dinner with friends tonight. I was playing a Matt Dennis tape in my car and planning supper. Fresh crabmeat, maybe, sautéed in olive oil and white wine with red and yellow and green peppers, and mushrooms, and served over rice. Or I could pound out some chicken thigh cutlets and marinate them in lemon juice and tarragon and a drop of virgin olive oil and cook them on my new Jenn-Air indoor grill. I could have a couple more beers while I waited for them to marinate, and I could eat them with some broccoli and maybe boiled red potatoes. I'd put a honey mustard dressing on the broccoli. Or maybe some tortellini . . . I parked in front of my place on Marlborough Street and went in. It was still and a little close. I opened the living room window a crack and ran through my choices again. I opted for the crab. Later there was a movie on cable, *Zulu,* one of my favorites. And the Celtics were playing Milwaukee, if I could stand any more basketball. The apartment echoed with a kind of spacious stillness, and the smell of spring evening seeped in through the open window. I'd been alone a lot in my life and I never tired of it.

"It's you, Dwayne," I said aloud. "You're shaving points."

I peeked in to see how the potatoes were doing in their pan, and shook the broccoli in its colander to get the last bits of water off.

"And shall I ruin your life by proving it?"

Nobody else said anything. So I added the crabmeat to the simmering pan and stirred it.

TEN

The next morning I went over to my office and typed up my notes from yesterday. I did pretty well with two fingers and some correction fluid, and by 11 A.M. I had a very convincing outline of the games in which Taft didn't make the spread, and what Dwayne Woodcock had done in each one.

It was a grand March day. The sun was bright yellow, the snow was gone, the wind still carried some chill, but around the base of the buildings, in bark mulched beds, crocuses were beginning to appear. *Nature's first green is crocus.* I had Dwayne's class schedule, and it told me he had an American History class that let out at one. I was at the door waiting when it did, but Dwayne wasn't one of the kids that came out. I strolled over to the cafeteria, where we'd had breakfast, but Dwayne wasn't there either.

I walked from the cafeteria to the President's

office and fixed my sensitive blue eyes on the
dread Ms. Merriman. I saw no signs of sexual
tension when I did so. Odd.

"Good afternoon, Ms. Merriman."

"Mr. Spenser."

"May I call you by your first name, Ms.
Merriman. We are, after all, destined to be
working closely on this matter."

"Are we really," Ms. Merriman said. "My
first name is June."

"June, do you suppose you could get me
Dwayne Woodcock's address?"

June did not ask me my first name; probably too shy.

"Mr. Spenser," she said, "I serve this President and this university and President Cort
has instructed me to help you as necessary.
But I also want you to know that I disapprove
personally, and very sincerely, of the degree
to which you are invading the privacy of one
of our students."

"Ah, June, 'tis a devious job I do. What
was that address?"

"I'll call the housing office," she said.
There was a little blush of red along her
cheekbones. She spent maybe two minutes on
the phone and when she hung up she handed
me a piece of notepaper with an address on it.

"He lives off campus," June said.

I took the paper. "Thanks, June. You don't

have a husband named Ward, do you?"

"I am not married," June said.

"Divorced?"

"Yes."

"Lot of that going around," I said. "N a fool."

"I don't believe my private life is pa this investigation, is it?"

"Good point," I said.

Dwayne Woodcock lived in a condominii complex a five-minute walk from the T. campus. It was a cluster of pseudo-Cape Co looking buildings of two or three storie asymmetrically jumbled at different heighi and angles, sided with weathered shingles with white trim and brightly colored fron doors. Dwayne's was cranberry. I rang the bell and in a minute Dwayne opened the door. He was barefoot and wearing gray sweat pants. His massive upper torso was shirtless.

"What do you want, man?"

"Got something to show you, Dwayne. Invite me in."

"What you got?"

"Not on the doorstep, Dwayne, for crissake. Show a little class."

Dwayne jerked his head and stepped away from the door. I went into a small entry hall with a staircase rising right. Straight ahead was the living room. On the coffee table in front of the white couch was a half gallon carton of orange juice. To my right a twenty-five-inch television set was on. Dwayne was watching *"Sonya Live in L.A."* To my left in an oversized green leather armchair was a black girl with corn rowed hair wearing a large maroon silk man's bathrobe. Her legs were tucked under her. She was drinking coffee from a large mug that had a picture of Opus the penguin on it. She held the mug in both hands and looked at me without expression across the top of it.

"Hello," I said.

She nodded behind the mug.

Dwayne didn't introduce us. "What you got to show me," he said.

"My name's Spenser," I said to the black girl.

"Chantel," she said.

"Nice to meet you, Chantel."

"Cut the bullshit, Spenser," Dwayne said. "What you got to show me?"

I handed him my outline.

"What's this?" Dwayne said.

"Read it," I said. "Then we'll talk."

Dwayne looked at the paper. I waited. Chantel sipped her coffee. Sonya and her guests chatted on and on. I looked at Dwayne. There was something funny about the way he looked at the paper. Suddenly I realized what it was. He wasn't moving his eyes. There were three sheets stapled together. He was still looking at the top sheet and his eyes weren't moving back and forth across the page as he read.

Finally Dwayne handed the typescript to Chantel.

"Here, babe, what you think of this?" he said.

Chantel took the paper with one hand and looked at it as she continued to sip from her coffee mug.

" 'Bout you, Dwayne," she said, " 'bout some games you played this year and what you did in them."

Dwayne turned his hard look on me again. "How come you writing stuff up about me?"

I had a suspicion. "You read it, Dwayne, it should be pretty clear."

"It pretty clear to you, Chantel?" Dwayne said.

"Dwayne, you know I don't know a lot about basketball." Chantel was reading more closely. She set her coffee mug down to turn the page, flipping it over its single staple and letting it hang down from the corner. "Say you didn't get a rebound in some game against B.C."

"Hey," Dwayne said, "how come you writing

that shit about Dwayne?"

"I love it when you refer to yourself in the third person," I said.

Dwayne frowned. "You gonna answer my question, man?"

"Dwayne," I said. "Can you read?"

"Dwayne Woodcock don't got to answer no bullshit questions from you, man."

"You can't, can you?" I said.

"Fuck off, man."

Dwayne was standing close to me, blocking the sun.

I ignored him and looked at Chantel. "He can't, can he, Chantel," I said.

Chantel said softly, "He can read a little. I'm trying to teach him."

"Shut up, Chantel. Don't tell this honkie motherfucker nothing."

Chantel's gaze was steady on Dwayne for a long moment. She opened her mouth and then decided not to speak and closed it. Dwayne turned toward me.

"You tell anybody 'bout this and I'm going to kill your motherfucking ass," he said.

"I shouldn't have to tell anyone, Dwayne. This is a goddamned college. You've been here four years. They should know."

"You hear what I'm saying?" Dwayne said.

"You and Chantel go over the stuff I gave you, Dwayne. It says when and how I think you shaved some points. When you've got it, and you want to talk about it, give me a call." I gave Chantel a card.

She looked at me with her steady gaze for a moment. "What you going to do?" she said. "You going to tell?"

"Never mind, Chantel. He ain't gonna do shit, he knows what's good for him." Dwayne put his hand on my shoulder to turn me toward him. I felt the little switch go that always went when people put their hands on me. I went with the direction Dwayne was trying to turn me, but I went much faster than he had in mind and as I came spinning around I brought my right arm up outside his and gave him a sharp chop with my forearm behind his elbow. With the force of my turning weight behind it, the blow slapped his arm across his chest like a loose tiller. I was right behind it and with my chest pressed against his flattened arm and my face very close to his chin, I said, "Don't make a bad mistake."

I could feel his body get rigid. I kept pressing against him. It pinned his right arm and I could feel what he was going to do before he did it.

"Hey, man," Dwayne said, "what's wrong with you?"

I looked up the nearly nine inches between my eyes and his. His eyes were soft. They

69

weren't scared. They were hurt. I stepped away, keeping my right foot back of my left, and my left shoulder turned slightly toward Dwayne. I could feel the air going in and out of my chest in big slow breaths.

"You crazy, man," Dwayne said, "fucking with Dwayne Woodcock? You crazy?" The voice was angry, street tough, Bed-Sty tough. But the eyes were hurt. The eyes were a kid who'd been startled and felt bad.

"No touching," I said. "You and Chantel talk and let me know." I stepped past Dwayne carefully and went out the front door and closed it softly behind me.

ELEVEN

"The kid can't read," I said to Susan. "He's a senior in college, carrying a C + average, and he can't read."

We were having dinner in Rocco's in the Transportation Building and I was halfway through a vodka martini on the rocks with a twist.

"You mentioned that," Susan said. "Twice on the ride over."

"It is outrageous," I said. "Nobody ever noticed?"

"Nobody ever cared," Susan said.

The waiter came to take our order. Susan decided on sweet and sour Thai soup and roast pheasant. I ordered black bean cake and Peking Duck.

"Isn't this the most spectacular room you've seen?" Susan said.

I nodded. "There's an academic adviser. Just for the team. Lot of major college teams

71

have them. Try to keep the kids on time to graduate and such."

Susan nodded encouragingly as she gazed around the high-ceilinged trompe l'oeil faux art decor.

"Academic adviser says Dwayne's intellectually gifted despite an impoverished childhood."

"Could be," Susan said.

"Sure, but the kid can't goddamn read. Don't you think someone might someplace make mention of that? He's twenty-one years old and in his senior year in college and he can't read."

"You mentioned that. Who are you mad at?"

I took a pleasing swallow of my martini. More than two and I got a headache, but one before dinner was just right, sometimes.

"I'm mad at his teachers, his academic counselor, him."

"Yes," Susan said. "Him too. He knows he can't read and hasn't corrected it."

"Hard for a kid like Dwayne to admit," I said.

"Yes," Susan said. "Maybe too hard. He needs help."

"There's a girlfriend, Chantel."

"Excuse me?"

"Chantel, she says she's trying to teach him."

Susan said, "Way back, first grade, second

grade, when he was trying to learn to read, he got passed over. He never broke the code."

"Meaning?"

The waiter brought the first course.

"Meaning that most of us learned to read phonetically. You can probably remember a teacher telling you to sound it out."

I nodded. The black bean cake had a slice of cob smoked ham on it, and a fried egg.

"For whatever reason, people who never learned to read never quite got the sound it out part. They know letters have sounds. Most can read a little. Words like *men, stop, rest room, beer,* words that they've seen so often they have become kind of pictographs. But they come to a word like, oh, *transportation,* and they are stuck. They try to make sense of the sounds a little," Susan did a halting imitation, "and then give up. They never learned the code and they never learned the rules. There are lots of rules, many of which we don't even think of."

"Like two vowels, separated by a consonant the first vowel is usually long . . . *sale, gale, pale,*" I said.

"Very good," Susan said. "Or the business that *ph* is normally pronounced like *f*. If you didn't know that you'd have an awful time. Of course he could be dyslexic."

"Can you be dyslexic and be the best basketball player in the country?" I said.

"Probably not," Susan said. "Frequently, though not always, dyslexia affects your balance. A standard dyslexia diagnostic test for kids is to ask them to walk a balance beam."

"Soup good?" I said.

"Yes, taste it," Susan said. She held out a spoonful and I slurped it in. I gestured at my bean cake. Susan smiled and shook her head.

"I haven't the heart," she said.

"No wonder I love you."

The waiter came by to ask if I wished another martini. I said no.

"So," Susan said, "what are you going to do, sweet cakes?"

"Eat all my Peking Duck as soon as it arrives," I said.

"What are you going to do about Dwayne and the point stuff and the fact that he can't read?"

"I was planning on consulting you for advice," I said.

The waiter took away our plates and brought the entrées.

"What's the girlfriend like?" Susan said. "Chanteuse."

"Chantel," I said. "Hard to say. I only saw her that once and most of the time I was seeing her, Dwayne was breathing fire on my neck."

74

"He is, I understand, six feet nine inches tall?"

"Yes."

"And he weighs in excess of two hundred and fifty pounds?"

I nodded.

"How's your neck?" Susan said.

"I was wearing my collar stylishly up, at the time," I said.

"Fashionable," Susan murmured, "yet practical."

I put a slice of duck on a pancake, brushed on the hoisin sauce with the scallion brush, put the scallion on top of the duck, folded the pancake over and took a bite. Not too big a bite. If I ate normally I always had my plate cleaned while Susan was still getting her knife and fork in position. Susan carefully cut a small piece of pheasant and moved it to her mouth and chewed slowly. She swallowed. I started a second pancake.

"I don't know what you should do about Dwayne," Susan said. "One option would be to do what you were hired to do."

"Report to the President that a viewing of the game films tells me that he shaved points in the following games?"

Susan nodded.

"Won't help the kid much."

"You weren't hired to help the kid."

"Kid grew up in one of the meanest ghettos in the world. He's gotten through almost four years at a major eastern university. He's going to have a pro career, unless he gets hurt, that will make him maybe a million dollars a year. Along the way he's acquired a nice girlfriend."

"And if you do what you're hired to do that all goes to hell," Susan said.

"Except maybe the girlfriend."

Susan smiled at me slowly. "That's what it really is, isn't it?" she said. "You are one of the three or four most romantic diddles in the world, and because this guy has a young woman who you think will stand by her man, you want to adopt them both."

"There's no such thing as a bad boy," I said.

"Sure," Susan said. "He ain't heavy, he's my brother." Her eyes were full of laughter, and something else, as she looked at me over the rim of her brandy alexander.

"A romantic diddle?"

"It's the first word that came to mind," she said.

"And yet you find me physically compelling."

"I find you compelling in every way," Susan said. And I knew what the something else was in her eyes.

76

"Even though I'm a romantic diddle?"

"Especially," Susan said, "because of that."

"So you agree that I should look into things a little more before I toot the whistle on the kid."

"I agree, I approve and, more than that, I knew before the conversation began that you weren't going to 'toot the whistle.' "

"Nobody likes a know-it-all," I said.

Susan put her hand out and laid it on top of mine. "Somebody does," she said.

TWELVE

I was sitting in my office with my feet up, thinking about Dwayne Woodcock and Chantel and point shaving and illiteracy and the backside of the new young paralegal who'd opened an office across the hall. The door to my office was open in case the paralegal wanted to stroll down the hall. A fine-looking black-haired man with a ruddy face walked in. He was wearing pale brown boaters and starched acid-washed jeans and a green polo shirt with the collar up. His jacket was silk tweed, dark brown and nipped in at the waist. His thick black hair was longish and brushed back on each side. A gold medallion on a thick gold chain showed at his throat. On his left hand was a big ring with a blue stone that looked like a high school or college ring. His sunglasses hung against his chest on a cord.

"How ya doing," he said when he came in.

"Fine," I said. I kept one eye peeled on the hallway.

"Got a few minutes?" he said.

"Sure." The accent was New York.

"Mind if I close the door?"

I sighed. "No," I said brightly, "go ahead."

He closed it and then turned and sat down in my client chair. He was about my height and slender. His hands were square and pale with a lot of black hair on the backs. The nails were manicured. I could smell cologne. There was a yellow silk handkerchief in the breast pocket of his jacket. He had the jacket sleeves pushed up over his forearms. On the left wrist was a gold Rolex.

"Nice office," he said.

"Compared to what?"

"Compared to working out of a packing crate in Canarsie," he said. "You mind if I smoke?"

I shook my head. He took a pigskin cigarette case out of his coat pocket, and a round gold lighter. He took out a cigarette, offered the open case to me. I shook my head. He snapped the case closed, dropped it into his side pocket, snapped a flame from the lighter, put the cigarette into his mouth and lit it, automatically shielding the flame as if the wind were blowing. He took in smoke and let it out through his nose as he dropped the

79

lighter back into the pocket with the cigarettes. Then he leaned back in the chair and stretched his feet in front of him and surveyed my office some more. He nodded approvingly.

"Nice little set up," he said.

I tried to look humble.

"Must make a pretty nice living with a set up like this."

I looked at the closed door.

I said, "I don't mean to seem impatient, but for the last hour I've been trying to get a look at the young woman across the hall and she usually walks by about this time."

He glanced over his shoulder at the closed door and then back at me, pausing a moment to figure out if he was being kidded. Then he grinned.

"Hey, pal, I never blame a man for hustling."

He took the cigarette out of his mouth oddly, with the palm facing away and the back of his hand closest to his face. He held the cigarette between his first two fingers, keeping the lighted end cupped slightly toward his palm.

"I'll make it quick," he said.

"Thank you," I said.

"We got a problem, you and me. Not the kind of problem can't be worked out. Couple of successful guys, a little good will, you scratch my back I scratch yours, everything is jake with a little effort."

I waited. He made himself even more comfortable in my client chair.

"My name is Bobby Deegan," he said.

I nodded.

"I'm in business in Brooklyn," Deegan said. "And I got some business interests up here."

I waited some more. He smoked some of his cigarette.

"Business been going good," he said, "and I'm showing a nice profit, but the interests up here are, ah . . . coming into conflict with your interests."

I leaned back on my spring chair and folded my hands across my stomach like Scattergood Baines and smiled.

Deegan smiled back at me.

"Dwayne Woodcock," he said.

"Dwayne Woodcock," I said.

We smiled happily at each other.

Outside in the corridor, through the closed door, I heard the sharp tap of high-heeled shoes walk past my door. Deegan heard it too.

"Balls," I said.

"Sorry," Deegan said.

"Always tomorrow," I said.

"With luck," Bobby Deegan said.

He let his gaze rest on me hard, steady, the hardcase stare. I waited.

After enough time Deegan laughed. "Big yard stare ain't going to do it, huh?"

"Been inside?" I said.

Bobby shrugged. It was a yes shrug. "So what are we going to do about Dwayne?" he said.

"I was thinking of teaching him to read," I said.

"He can't read?" Deegan said.

"No," I said.

Deegan shook his head and made a silent whistle. "Any other plans?"

I was getting tired of people asking me what I was going to do about Dwayne Woodcock.

"I don't know," I said. I'd read somewhere that if you were patient and didn't get mad and let people talk eventually they'd say something. I was skeptical, but I was experimenting.

Deegan looked around for an ashtray, saw one on the top of my file cabinet, stood, walked over, and stubbed out the cigarette.

"Don't smoke yourself, huh?" he said.

"Quit in 1963," I said.

"Good for you," Deegan said. "I been trying for a couple of years."

I didn't say anything.

"You're not helping," Deegan said.

"No," I said. "I'm not."

"Okay, he said. "It can go a couple of ways. One way is we give you a nice fee for deciding that Dwayne isn't shaving anything but his face. The college likes that, Dwayne likes that, Coach likes that, we like it. Nobody doesn't like it." Deegan gave me a big grin.

"And the other way?"

"We put you in the ground," Deegan said. His voice was pleasant.

"Eek," I said.

"Sure, sure," Deegan said. "I know you're tough. We talked to a couple guys we know up here. But think about it. What's worth dying for here? You take Dwayne down, you ruin a kid's life that ain't got many options. And you probably get killed in the deal. Who gets hurt if you walk around it? You get some bread for your trouble. Dwayne gets to be a big star in the NBA instead of a small time hoodlum in Bed-Sty. And who gets hurt? Team wins that should win, fans are happy. You think the college wants you to find out that there's points being shaved? Dwayne's a good kid, pal. Why fuck him up?"

"How much you willing to give me?" I said.

Deegan glanced around my office again. "Two bills," he said.

I shook my head.

"How much you want?" Deegan said.

"Two hundred thirty-eight billion," I said.

Deegan was silent for a moment, then he grinned slowly. "Well, like the old joke, we've established what you are, now we're just haggling over price."

"Be a long haggle," I said.

Deegan nodded. "Option two's looking better," he said.

We sat for a moment quietly while Deegan lit another cigarette.

"So what are you going to do?" Deegan said.

"Hell, Bobby, I don't know. I was trying to figure that out when you came in and distracted me."

"I thought you was trying to get a look at some broad's ass," Deegan said.

"That too," I said.

Deegan rose. "Okay, pal. You think about it some more, and I'll check back with you. Try not to be too fucking stupid."

"I been trying for years," I said. "Usually it doesn't work out."

Deegan laughed and walked to the door. He opened it and stopped and looked back at me.

"You know we mean it," he said.

"Sure," I said.

Deegan shrugged and started out.

"Leave the door open," I said. "I didn't hear her come back yet."

THIRTEEN

Maybe a minute after Deegan left, the paralegal across the hall came back from wherever she'd been. *Worth the wait.*

I put my feet up on my desk and looked at the toes of my Reeboks. *Okay.* I knew that Dwayne was shaving points for some New York guys of whom Bobby Deegan was one. Maybe Danny Davis. Deegan hadn't mentioned him, but he had no reason to. I hadn't talked to Davis. Bobby had no reason to think he was a suspect. But the kid at the school paper had said the story source was somebody's girlfriend, and I was willing to bet it hadn't been Chantel. Which meant at least one of the others was in on it. *So what?* If I decided to take Dwayne down, anyone else involved would have to go down too. If I let Dwayne off, they got off too. No point thinking about them at the moment. The thing was, a lot of Deegan's arguments were right. Some bookies took a bath, but otherwise nobody much suffered from point shaving. The integrity of the game maybe suffered, but that was too abstract for me.

Outside my door the corridor was still. All around me people were working away on bills of sale, and order forms and service calls. No one had time to be hanging around the corridor, not if they were going to get ahead, or be number one, or not get fired. Actually it was probably Dwayne who got hurt. Shaving points couldn't do much for your self-respect unless you got a good feeling from slipping one by the establishment. It would make a guy like Deegan feel good. He was a nearly ideal wiseguy. He'd love the shiftiness, the hustle of it, the smart money he was making. I didn't think Dwayne was like Deegan . . . *He might want to be.* Who knew. So was I going to bust Dwayne for his own good? *Hurts me more than it does you, Dwayne.*

"Shit," I said.

I owed Baron Morton and Taft University the job I'd agreed to do when they hired me. I owed Dwayne Woodcock nothing. He was an arrogant kid, but he was sullen. *Okay. So I don't turn the kid in.*

I got up and looked out my office window at the still bleak spring. Berkeley Street was washed in a pale yellow sun. On the corner of

Boylston, opposite me, a young woman walked with two short gray woolly dogs on a pair of leashes. She held the leashes in one hand and carried a pooper scooper in the other. The task was a challenge to her. The dogs, who looked straight from a Disney movie, were crisscrossing in front of her tangling their leashes, and the young woman was trying to untangle them without letting go of the pooper scooper.

"You think you've got problems," I said.

I sat back down and began admiring the toes of my shoes again. I couldn't just walk away from it. I couldn't blow the whistle on Dwayne yet, but I couldn't leave Deegan and company in place either, and there was the matter of literacy. I figured Deegan wouldn't try to shoot me for the moment. If I was killed while investigating point shaving it would produce just the result they were trying to avoid. If they were logical. I picked up the Taft file from my desk and flipped through it looking at my notes. Madelaine Roth, Ph.D.

I got up and put on my leather jacket and went out and closed the office door behind me. When in doubt do something; and hope that if you keep doing it you'll come to understand what it is. Across the hall the door to the paralegal office was open. She was at her desk thumbing through *The Harvard Law Review*.

She looked up as I stepped out of my office, and smiled. I smiled back and gave her the kind of wave where you hold your hand still and wiggle your fingers. She wiggled back.

Enthralled.

FOURTEEN

Madelaine Roth had high cheekbones and very pale skin and a mass of auburn hair. She sat in her office wearing a dark blue silk dress splattered with red flowers, crossed her legs and let her swivel chair tilt back behind her big blond desk. The wall was covered with pictures of the Taft basketball team, clippings, letters from former players and announcements of summer tutorial offerings, new courses, new academic regulations and her three degrees, each separately framed in blond wood that matched her desk. There were bookcases on two walls filled mostly with paperback books that had the look of required reading. Her desktop was covered with papers. Her big round blue-rimmed glasses lay among the papers. There were two ballpoint pens and a red pencil among the papers as well.

"I read the article in the student newspaper,

89

Mr. Spenser," she said. "And really, unfounded allegations, rumors, unnamed sources. It is simply amazing how much these students refuse to learn."

"Amazing in fact," I said. "Did you ever notice that Dwayne Woodcock can't read?"

Madelaine's face flushed and her dark blue eyes rounded and then narrowed almost at once.

"I beg your pardon," she said.

"I said have you ever noticed that Dwayne Woodcock can't read?"

She shook her head. Her face was still flushed.

"That's, that's simply, ah, crazy. Dwayne's a senior in college, of course he can read. Why on earth would you say he can't."

"I gave him a few pages of typescript to read and he couldn't read it."

"Well, for heaven's sake, it's like the old voter literacy tests in Mississippi, you ask someone to read a complicated technical report and when they can't, or perhaps simply won't, you assume they're illiterate."

"It was a discussion of several basketball games in which he played," I said.

Her face was very red now, and she shook her head firmly. "Literacy testing is quite a complex specialty, Mr. Spenser. I suspect that you were not entirely qualified. I wonder

90

if Dwayne were white if you'd be so quick to assume illiteracy."

"Some of my best friends are jigaboos," I said.

Dr. Roth looked like she'd swallowed a hairbrush.

"Mr. Spenser, I assume you're trying to joke; but the racial cliché is offensive."

"I'm feeling offensive, Dr. Roth. I am sitting here being bullshitted in patronizing tones, and we both know you know he's illiterate."

"I'm afraid that's enough, Mr. Spenser. You'll have to leave." Madelaine spoke with as much dignity as one could who was blushing scarlet.

"That's silly, Madelaine," I said. "This is a testable hypothesis. Kicking me out won't protect you from embarrassment when Dwayne's illiteracy becomes public knowledge and people ask you how come you're writing these rave reviews of his academic performance."

"I feel no embarrassment in trying to help a poor black boy to stay in school. Would you have me send him back to the ghetto?"

"So you know he can't read," I said.

"I know his skills are not, perhaps, what they should be, granted, but would he be better off back in that environment? The boy has a future here."

"He'd probably rather be called a man," I said.

"I know about calling black people 'boy,' " Madelaine said. "But he is a boy."

"Not on a basketball court," I said.

"But otherwise," Madelaine said. "He's not a grown man. He's a boy."

"Why do you say so?" I said.

"For God's sake," Madelaine said. "He can't even read."

I smiled. Madelaine looked at me, puzzled; why was I smiling? I smiled some more. The room was quiet. Madelaine frowned. Then the light went on. Had she not been flushed she would have flushed.

"Well, not just because he can't read," Madelaine said. It was weak, and she knew it, but like a lot of academics I had met she kept chewing at it. She was so used to manipulating meaning with language that both became relative. As if you could make falsehood true by richly said restatement. Academics are not first rate at saying *I was wrong*.

"What are the other aspects of his boyness?" I said, finally.

Madelaine opened her mouth, closed it, took a long breath. "This is pointless," she said. "I do not have the time to sit here and argue with some redneck detective."

"We're not arguing, Dr. Roth. I'm trying to educate you, and you're resisting. We can't just let Dwayne's illiteracy go," I said, "because we think he won't need to be able to read or because we think he can't or won't learn. Those assumptions, Doc, are racist, and it's what's wrong with this whole deal. This kid has gone through sixteen years of education, public and private, and he can't read, and no one has bothered about that."

"You just called him a kid," Madelaine said. She was sullen now.

"He is a kid. He hasn't got the shrewdness or the strength to admit he can't read and get help so that he can. He thinks he's going to make so much dough playing basketball that he won't ever have to read. He'll get a smart agent. And he'll be entirely dependent on him. And when Dwayne's about thirty-four, thirty-five, he won't be making any more money playing basketball, and so he won't have an agent and then what's he going to do? Manage his affairs?"

"But you were dreadful to me when I called him a boy."

"Dreadful's a little strong," I said.

"I'm not a racist," she said.

"What's in a name," I said. "But when I came in here, I wasn't sure what to do with Dwayne. Now I am. And it's you that showed me. I'm going to treat him like a man."

"Does that mean you're going to turn him in?" Madelaine said.

"I don't know," I said. "But whatever I do I'm going to treat him like he's responsible for himself and his life."

"And what about me?" she said.

"What about you?"

"Are you going to tell that he can't read?"

I stared at her.

"It would be very hurtful to my professional standing," she said.

She was leaning forward in her chair now, her hands resting on the edge of her desk. Her mouth was open and her tongue moved rapidly back and forth over her lower lip.

I was still staring.

"Holy Christ," I said.

FIFTEEN

Hawk and I tried to have dinner together once a week or so just as if we were regular people. After a session with Madelaine Roth, Hawk looked a lot more regular to me than he used to. We had a table against the wall in a storefront place called the East Coast Grill in Inman Square, where all the cooking was done over an open barbecue pit in the back, by a guy in a red baseball cap. I ordered the ribs, Hawk asked for grilled tuna.

"Don't dare order the ribs, do you?" I said.

"Heard it came with a wedge of watermelon," Hawk said.

"Your national cuisine," I said.

We were drinking Lone Star beer, in respect to the barbecue, and the first one went quickly. As we drank, people glanced covertly at Hawk. He was wearing white leather pants and a black silk shirt. His shaved head gleamed, and his movements were almost balletic:

economical and surgically exact. He never moved for no reason. He never spoke to make conversation. His white leather jacket hung on the back of the chair, and if you paid attention to stuff like that, you could see where it hung a little lopsided from the weight of the gun in the right hand pocket. When he brought the beer glass to his lips you could see the muscles in his upper arm swell, stretching the silk of his shirt sleeve. The waitress brought us a second beer.

Hawk said, "Guy named Bobby Deegan came by to see me."

"Bobby gets around," I said.

"You know him?" Hawk said.

"Came by my office this morning," I said. "Urged me to lay off a thing I was looking into."

"S'pose you said, 'sho nuff, Bobby,'" Hawk said.

"I was going to," I said. "But my chin was trembling so bad it was hard to talk."

"Ah," Hawk said. "That why Bobby looking to have you clipped."

"Clipped?"

"Un huh."

"A sweetie like me?"

"Un huh."

"Gee," I said. "I thought I'd won him over."

"Guess not," Hawk said. "Bobby come in to Henry's looking for me. Said he needed some pest removal work done. Heard I was in that business."

I shook my head. "Pest removal," I said. "That hurts."

"Can see why it would," Hawk said.

The waitress came and brought ribs for me and tuna for Hawk. On the plate with my ribs were some beans, some watermelon and a big piece of cornbread.

Hawk looked at the slab of ribs. "Mighta made an error," Hawk said.

"Tuna's good for you," I said.

"Sure," Hawk said. "So I ask Bobby where he heard that, and he said, guy he'd done some business with in town. I say 'gimme a name.' He say . . . " Hawk smiled happily, " 'Gerry Broz.' "

I said, "A blast from the past."

Hawk cut a morsel off his tuna and inspected it. It was pink, as promised. Hawk nodded his head once and put the tuna into his mouth and chewed. He nodded once again, and swallowed.

"So I figure the guy's probably straight, using Joe's kid's name, anybody can know Joe's, but most folks don't know 'bout Gerry."

"So I say what's the pest's name, and he say you."

I was struggling happily with my ribs. Normally I ended up with barbecue sauce in my socks when I ate ribs, but I always figured they were worth it.

"What's he paying?" I said when I could.

"Five bills," Hawk said.

"For crissake," I said, "Harry Cotton was offering that, when, seven, eight years ago."

"Yeah, well, Bobby's out of town, he don't know 'bout you. So, I say, 'You tell Gerry who you want hit?' And he say, 'No, what's the difference?' and I say, 'No difference.' "

Hawk ate a couple of grilled vegetables. I ate some beans. Hawk drank some beer, patted his lips carefully with his napkin, put it back on his lap.

"So Bobby say, 'Well?' And I say, 'Well what?' and Bobby say, 'You want the job?' and I say, 'no.' And Bobby say, 'How come?' and I just look at him for a while and Bobby say, 'Well, okay, fine, you don't want it.' And I just looking at him and he say, 'You got any suggestions?' and I say, 'no' and Bobby takes a walk."

I shook my head. "Five grand," I said. "That's insulting."

"Hey," Hawk said, "I just reporting the news."

I nodded. My ribs were gone, also the beans and the watermelon and the cornbread.

Also my beer. I'd done another good job at the table.

"These are serious guys," I said. "Bobby came into my office this morning, offered a bribe, made a threat, neither one worked, so he went right out and found you."

"And when I said no he probably went on and found somebody else not as good," Hawk said. He was working on his supper now that it was my turn to talk.

"The only one as good would be me," I said, "and I wouldn't do it either."

"Still, they probably find some people willing," Hawk said. "Not everybody know better."

"Sucker born every minute," I said.

"What you into?" Hawk said.

"Basketball," I said.

"The national sport," Hawk said, "of ma people. Better tell me about it."

I did. While I did, Hawk finished his meal, the waiter came and cleared it and brought dessert menus.

"The bread pudding with whiskey sauce," I said to Hawk.

Hawk held up two fingers to the waiter and said, "Bread pudding."

We were eating the pudding by the time I got to Madelaine Roth. And I finished with Madelaine and the pudding at about the same time.

"What you think 'bout Bobby," Hawk said when I got through.

"I think that cheerful, pally act is a very thin veneer over a very tough guy," I said.

Hawk nodded. "Yeah," he said. "How 'bout I cruise around with you a while. Might meet me some adventurous coeds."

"Yeah," I said, "might be able to help me get Dwayne's attention too."

"Or Chantel's," Hawk said.

"Hawk," I said, "Dwayne is, you gotta remember, approximately the size of Harlem."

"There's that," Hawk said.

"Besides, I think we're trying to help him," I said.

"What's this we, white man? You the helper, I just along to see how it goes."

"Mr. Warm," I said.

The waiter brought the check. Hawk picked it up, looked at it and handed it to me.

SIXTEEN

The next time I went to see Dwayne Wood-cock, Hawk came with me. We found Dwayne in the spa in the Student Union drinking a Coke in a booth with two other kids. I recognized them. One was Kenny Green, the off guard, and a reserve forward named Daryl Pope. Dwayne looked up and said something to the other two. There was some laughter.

"Dwayne," I said. "We need to talk."

Dwayne was playing to his friends. "I don't need to talk, man. You need to talk whyn't you go someplace and talk?" He made the last word stretch. Hawk came up and leaned against the corner of the booth. All three kids looked at Hawk uneasily.

"I had a chat with Bobby Deegan," I said.

Everyone at the table got a little stiffer when I said Deegan's name.

"I don't know nobody by that name, man," Dwayne said. "Sounds like some dumb fucking Irishman to me."

Dwayne's buddies laughed along with him.

"Don't that sound like that to you?" Dwayne said.

"Sounds like that to me," one of his buddies said.

I looked at Hawk. I was getting tired of college kids. Dwayne was especially easy to get tired of.

"Want me to shoot one?" Hawk said.

All three turned and looked at him.

"Who you talking to, man?" Dwayne said.

Hawk turned his head slowly and looked at him, carefully. Then he looked at the other two, just as carefully.

Basketball players are big, and it's been years since they were reedy. There was nothing in Hawk's look that I could see that was anything but neutrally interested. He didn't say anything. But when he was through looking at them, all three kids had stopped laughing. Green and Pope looked at Dwayne, he looked back at Hawk for a minute, and then looked at me.

"You bring some fucking dude around, say he's going to shoot us?"

"Dude," I said to Hawk.

"Talks like all those bad-ass black guys on television, don't he," Hawk said.

102

"Heart of the ghetto," I said, "pulse beat of the streets."

Hawk leaned a little forward toward Dwayne and spoke softly.

"You had best excuse yourself from your friends, young man, and allow us to speak with you. We have your best interest at heart."

Hawk's eyes were steady on Dwayne.

Finally Dwayne said, "Man, shit. I may's well get this over. You guys give us couple minutes. Get these fucking people out of my hair."

"We be over at the counter, Dwayne," Pope said.

"Sure," Dwayne said. "I'll catch you in a minute."

When they were gone I slid into the booth opposite Dwayne. Hawk sat beside me.

"Whatcha want?" Dwayne said.

"I think I want to help you," I said.

"Dwayne don't need help. Dwayne can carry the weight, you know?"

"What weight you carrying, Dwayne?"

"Whatever fuckin' weight you think you going to talk about. Dwayne Woodcock don't need no motherfucking help, man."

"You need help, Dwayne," I said. "You can't read, and you can't write, and some hard guys from New York got hold of your balls."

"Bullshit, man . . . "

"You don't think they got hold of your balls. You think you're making some easy bread, and no one gets hurt. But one of these days you'll try to walk away, and, whoa, sonovagun, they got a firm grip on your nads, and they're starting to squeeze."

"Nobody gonna squeeze Dwayne's balls," he said, "no dumb Irish fucker like Deegan. No honkie motherfucker like you, either."

Dwayne took a big breath. "Don't need advice from no honkie motherfucker, either," he said.

"Yes you do," Hawk said. "You need advice wherever you can find it." His voice was quiet. "And this is about the best place. It's also about the last place. You don't get help, and pretty soon advice ain't going to matter. You going to belong to Bobby Deegan, or the cops. Or you going to be dead."

"Whyn't you just leave this alone," Dwayne said.

Hawk's voice was still soft. "He ain't going to do that. He doesn't leave things alone. You can trust him. You can trust me. Lot of men don't meet two people they can trust in their whole lives."

Dwayne didn't say anything. He just shook his head. Hawk and I were silent. Pope and Green stood at the counter, looking at us, ready

104

to jump in. Dwayne kept shaking his head.

I waited.

Finally Dwayne said, "Bobby say he was going to talk with you."

I nodded. Next to me Hawk was in absolute repose. His hands on the table before him were perfectly still. He was looking at Dwayne. He had an expression of mild interest.

"Bobby say he going to talk with you and take care of it."

"He didn't take care of it," I said.

"He will," Dwayne said, and got up, which in itself was fairly impressive, and walked out of the spa with his two buddies in trail.

I looked at Hawk.

"Big," he said.

"From the neck down," I said.

Hawk shrugged. "You could turn him in," he said.

I shook my head.

Hawk grinned. "Figured that would be too simple for you."

Classes broke and a swarm of undergraduates filled the spa. Hawk and I left the booth and pushed through them out onto the quadrangle.

"Where's Gerry in this deal?" I said.

"Broz?"

"Yeah. He sent Deegan to you."

"Figure Deegan's from New York," Hawk said.

"And he knows Gerry Broz," I said.

"Maybe we ought to find out how," Hawk said.

"Joe won't like that," I said.

Hawk grinned again. "Yikes," he said.

"Makes your blood run cold, doesn't it," I said. "But once we find out what's it going to do for me?"

"Know that when we find out," Hawk said.

I nodded.

"What else you got?"

I shrugged. "Got Dixie," I said.

"The coach? Thought he found you annoying."

"Hard to believe, isn't it," I said. "But he can put pressure on the kid that you and I can't."

Hawk's face brightened. "By sitting him down," Hawk said.

"Yes. If I can persuade Dixie to bench Dwayne until he cooperates we might have something."

"Means you've got to convince Dixie that Dwayne's doing what you say," Hawk said.

"And Dixie would rather get a case of clap than talk to me," I said.

"Amen to that," Hawk said.

SEVENTEEN

I walked into Dixie Dunham's office in the gym on a March morning that felt like January. There was snow, and wind and a windchill factor. I had the lining zipped back into my leather jacket.

"What the fuck are you doing here?" Dixie said when he saw me.

I put my gym bag down on his desk and took the game tapes out of it. I put them on the desk in front of him. They were the six games where Taft beat the spread. I took out a copy of the running transcript that Tommy Christopher and I had put together.

"Read that," I said, "and watch the tapes and you'll know that Dwayne Woodcock's influencing the point spread."

"Where'd you get those tapes? I didn't authorize those tapes to anyone."

"I showed the transcript to Dwayne and he couldn't read it," I said.

"I told you, you sonovabitch, I told you to stay away from my players." Dixie shoved his swivel chair back behind his desk and stood up. "You trying to rig this goddamn tournament, come in here and fuck with my players' heads? You bastard, you're the one rigging the spread. I told you, I explicitly fucking told you . . ."

"Goddamn it, Dixie," I said, "shut up."

Dixie was so startled that someone would say that to him that he shut up. For a moment.

I charged into that moment. "You got a kid here, he's not just one of your players, he's also a real actual kid, and he's in trouble and you don't give a rat's ass about it. You're so goddamned busy being a coaching legend that you're going to let him slide right into the sewer."

Dixie's face was red.

"People don't talk to me that way," he said. His voice was tight as if he had trouble forcing it through his throat.

"People don't usually talk to you any way," I said. "You're such a goddamned windbag they don't get a chance."

Dixie came around the corner of the desk in a rush and threw a looping right-handed punch at me. It was like watching the slow curving swoop of a Frisbee. When it got close I turned my head to the left and let his fist soar majestically on past. Then I drove a left hook into his solar plexus, turning on the ball of my right foot and getting a lot of my weight behind it.

Dixie said "oof," and he folded like a camp stool and staggered back against his desk trying to get his breath.

I didn't say anything. I waited. Dixie got enough wind in him in a short time to lunge off the desk at me again. As he came I took a quick shuffle step left and put a right hook into the same spot, pivoting this time the other way and getting even more weight behind it. Dixie staggered back, doubled over again, leaned against the desk and then slid slowly to the floor, his legs stretching out before him with no strength in them, a look of puzzlement on his face. I knew the feeling. Dixie sat there, his arms wrapped across his stomach, bent forward, trying to get air, for maybe a full minute, while I waited without saying anything. Finally he could breathe. He put both hands flat on the floor and supported himself while he sat straighter, still on the floor, and his eyes began to focus on me.

"You got a punch like a mule," Dixie said.

"Like the kick of a mule," I said. "Get it right."

Dixie nodded without speaking. Then he pulled his legs toward him and twisted and got them under him and rose to one knee, holding on to the desk, rested a minute and then boosted himself up onto both feet and stood there, leaning forward, his hands palm down on his desk, his shoulders hunched, his back to me. He breathed for a while and then finally rolled himself around along the desk edge until he had turned and faced me. He put one hand up, palm out.

"Ain't going to try again," he said. "Just getting my legs back."

I waited.

"Hoooeee," Dixie said.

"Yeah," I said.

"You warned me," he said.

"Yeah."

Dixie took a couple of deep breaths and arched his back. Then he went around his desk and got his chair and sat in it.

"Okay," he said. "What were you saying about Dwayne going down the chute?"

"Read the transcript," I said.

Dixie picked it up, opened his drawer, took out a pair of horn-rimmed half glasses, put them low on his nose and started to put his feet up. He stopped suddenly just after he started and put them back on the floor, and opened the folder and started to read. While he read, I looked around the room. It was classic gym cinder block, painted white.

There was a picture of Dixie with Troy Murphy, who'd been an all-American point guard for Dixie and was now a star with the Portland Trail Blazers. But there weren't any others. No team pictures, no memorabilia. In the corner across from Dixie's desk was a big screen television set and a VCR on a yellow oak table. Three or four folding chairs leaned against the wall. I looked back at Dixie. He had one page flipped over and was reading the second one. I waited. Dixie flipped the second page. His face had no expression. Somewhere, faintly echoing off the cinder block, I could hear a basketball pounding on a floor.

Dixie finished the typescript. He put it down on his desk, reached out and assembled the videocassettes in a neat pile, stood carefully, and walked somewhat stiffly, carrying the tapes to the VCR. He arranged them in order, turned on the VCR and the TV, put a cassette into the VCR, punched PLAY and walked back, slowly, to his desk. He lowered himself carefully into his chair and leaned back and began to watch the videotape. I leaned on the wall and watched it too, for maybe the fifth time.

Dixie watched the tapes, the way he'd read the transcript. There was no expression on his face. He had no reaction. He didn't say a word. When the first tape was over, he started to push himself up.

"Stay," I said. "I'll run the machine."

Dixie settled back into his chair. I went to the VCR and changed cassettes. When the last one was finished, it was midafternoon. I picked all the cassettes up and put them into the gym bag. Dixie still sat. Neither one of us made a sound. I went back to leaning on the wall. After a while Dixie swiveled his chair toward me.

"Dwayne's shaving points," Dixie said. "Maybe Danny Davis, too."

I nodded.

"You see what you want to see, I guess," Dixie said. "You say he can't read."

I nodded.

"Shit," Dixie said.

I leaned on the wall some more. Dixie sat. The sound of basketballs bouncing had stopped.

"What we going to do?" Dixie said. "East regionals start next Saturday."

"I don't know for sure what we're going to do," I said. "But I've got some goals. One, the kid's involved with New York wiseguys and I want to get him unhooked from them. Two, I want to be able to preserve his future. Three, I want him to learn to read."

"If we turn him in, his future is zero," Dixie said. "Pros won't touch him."

"I know," I said.

"Means you're going to cover up for him?"

"Yeah, I guess it does," I said. "How about you?"

Dixie shook his head. "He's the best player I ever had. Better than Troy, even." Dixie jerked his head toward the picture on the wall.

I waited.

"People can't trust the score, any game goes to hell," he said.

I shifted shoulders against the wall.

"I don't know," Dixie said. "I don't know what to do."

"Let's take it a step at a time," I said. "Let's talk with the kid. If he'll admit it, then we can move on the guys who rigged him to do it."

"What if he denies it?" Dixie said.

"You tell him you looked at the tapes, you know he did it. If he still won't admit anything, you sit him down."

"Sit him down?" Dixie said the words very slowly, with space between them.

"Yeah."

"For how long?"

"Until he tells us what's going on. Until he names names."

"Jesus Christ," Dixie said. "I got the East regionals next week. We get through those I got the tourney at Salt Lake. In about three weeks I could be playing for the national championship."

"I didn't say my plan was fun," I said.

"Fun, my God. Can't we use the tapes for proof?"

"Probably not in court, but even so, we don't want to go to court. And if we did, what have we got? The fact that Dwayne, maybe Danny Davis, is shaving points. We don't have for whom. And *for whom* is what we need if we're going to pull this off without screwing the kid."

"So what are you going to do if he does tell you?" Dixie said. "You say you don't want to ruin the kid, so you can't go to the cops."

"Dixie," I said, "you got to understand this kind of work. I don't have a game plan. I sort of feel my way along. When I run into something I don't know, I try to find out. When I find out enough, then maybe there's a way to figure out what to do. And maybe there isn't. You can't know until you find out what there is to find out."

Dixie rocked slowly in his swivel chair. His hands were folded across his stomach, and he seemed to be studying his thumbnails. Finally, without looking up, Dixie said, "I'll talk with Dwayne."

I said, "You want me around?"

"No."

"Okay," I said. "Let me know."

"Yeah, I will."

I picked up my gym bag and started out the door.

"Spenser," Dixie said.

I stopped and turned my head.

"I didn't know he couldn't read," Dixie said.

"Makes you wonder how he maintained a two point three average, doesn't it," I said.

"Maybe we ought to find that out too," Dixie said.

"We will," I said.

EIGHTEEN

Tuesday morning, Hawk and I went to see Gerry Broz. Gerry was a second generation thug, been to college, graduated into the old man's business. He spent every morning in a coffee shop near Oak Square in Brighton. He'd have breakfast, read the paper, drink some coffee, make a few phone calls, receive a few visitors. Joe still ran things, but Gerry was the crown prince.

"Joe's garbage," Hawk said as we were walking across Washington Street toward the B&D Coffee Shop. "And Gerry's nowhere near the man Joe is."

"I know," I said. "Cops will be glad when Gerry takes over. They figure the organization will turn into pot shards in about a year."

"Pot shards," Hawk said.

We opened the door to the coffee shop and went in. The air was steamy with the scent of coffee and bacon and cigarette smoke. There

116

was a rusty-colored marble counter and four booths by the big front window. The place looked as if it had originally been built to be a variety store and been converted, home style, by either B or D or maybe both.

Gerry was in his booth, farthest from the door by the window. There was a thick guy with curly black hair sitting opposite him with his overcoat on.

The first time I met Gerry he was still an undergraduate, selling coke and blackmailing women when he wasn't studying for midterms. Now he was about twenty-seven and looked younger. He had a soft face and a limp black mustache. He'd put on some weight, none of it sinew, and he hadn't adjusted his wardrobe, so that while he wore very expensive clothes they were a little tight everywhere.

He spotted us when we came in and said something to the man across from him. The man across from him put one hand inside his coat as he turned and looked at us over his shoulder.

"What do you want, creep?" Gerry said.

"Gee, Gerry," I said, "getting porky hasn't improved your style any, has it?"

The man across from him had twisted himself around in the booth with one leg resting in the seat, so that he was fully facing us.

Hawk stepped up to the counter and ordered two coffees.

"The gentleman there wants it on his tab," Hawk said. The counter woman nodded and shuffled after the coffee.

"I asked you a question," Gerry said.

"Commendable," I said. "So many people these days are always talking *me, me, me,* but you've developed listening skills. You're a sensitive guy, Ger."

Hawk came over with a cup of coffee in a Styrofoam cup. I took it and had a small sip. Hawk went back and sat on a stool at the counter and leaned one elbow on the counter and watched.

"Love a Styrofoam cup, don't you, Ger?"

"Spenser, I know you think you're a fucking scream, but I don't, and I'm a busy man. You got something to say to me, say it. And get the fuck out of here."

"I want to talk with you, Gerry. Unlike everybody else in the world."

"Talk," Gerry said.

"Tell your gunboat to beat it," I said. "It's just me and you."

Gerry shrugged. He made a hand gesture at the counter.

"Over there, Jojo," he said. "For a minute."

Jojo slid out of the booth carefully, his hand still under his coat, his eyes flickering back

118

and forth between me and Hawk. He took a stool beside Hawk.

"How's it going," Hawk said pleasantly.

Jojo shrugged. I slid into the booth across from Gerry.

"Okay, what do you want?" Gerry said.

"Bobby Deegan," I said.

"Who's he?"

It was a standard reaction for a guy like Gerry. If I'd said George Washington he'd have said the same thing. College hadn't helped Gerry all that much.

"My question exactly," I said.

"Why ask me?"

"Because Bobby mentioned your name to my associate," I tipped my head toward Hawk, "and suggested you were a tight personal friend."

Gerry raised both hands in front of him palm out.

"Never heard of the guy," he said.

"Bobby says he asked you to point him at a good hitter, and you sent him to Hawk."

Gerry pushed out his lower lip and shook his head.

"I was supposed to be the hittee," I said.

There was a little movement in Gerry's eyes for a moment and then nothing.

"Would I send a guy to Hawk if he wanted

you hit?" Gerry said. "How stupid you think I am?"

"Awful stupid," I said. "Bobby didn't tell you who he wanted hit."

"Look, asshole," Gerry said. "I told you I don't know nothing about no Bobby Deegan. You unnerstand? Nothing."

"Gerry," I said, "I've known you since you were a boy."

"You're a pain in the ass. You been a pain in the ass to the old man and you're a pain in the ass to me. The old man let it slide. I don't know why. He does what he does. But I ain't going to let it slide. You hear me talking? You get in my way and you're going to sleep with the fishes." Gerry's voice was soft, but he leaned forward and his face was reddish-looking as he spoke.

I turned toward the counter.

"Hawk, you hear this conversation?" I said.

Hawk shook his head.

"Gerry says if I get in his way I'm going to sleep with the fishes."

Hawk's quiet face broke into a slow widening grin.

"Sleep with the fishes?" he said.

I was smiling too. "Yeah."

Hawk began to chuckle quietly and then to laugh and finally he bent over on his stool and pressed his hands against his stomach and laughed.

"Sleep with the fishes," he said, his voice shaking. "Sleep with the fucking fishes."

There was a slim black guy who looked like a cabbie sitting next to Hawk at the counter, and in another booth there were two Irish-looking women, who had probably walked the kids to school and were on their way home. All three studiously ignored the hilarity.

"Guppies," I said to Gerry, "could I sleep with some guppies? I always sort of liked guppies."

Gerry was redder than before. He jerked his head at Jojo and said, "Let's get the fuck out of here."

Jojo slid off the stool and stood by the booth as Gerry edged out of the booth and stood up.

"Does this mean you're not going to tell me about Bobby Deegan?" I said.

"Fuck you," Gerry said, and stomped out of the coffee shop. Jojo barely got to the door in time to hold it for him. Through the window I saw them get into a charcoal gray Mercedes sedan, Jojo behind the wheel, and drive away.

Hawk got off the stool and stood beside me looking through the window.

"Not productive," I said.

"Counterproductive," Hawk said. "Now we got to worry about Bobby Deegan putting a hit on you cause you screwing up his scam, and we got to worry about Gerry putting a hit on you cause you hurt his feelings."

"Had to ask," I said.

"Sure," Hawk said.

"Hurting Gerry Broz's feelings isn't a bad day's work," I said.

"True," Hawk said.

NINETEEN

I was back on paralegal watch when Chantel knocked on the frame of the open door. I put my feet on the floor and stood.

"Come in," I said.

She was wearing black stockings and a red leather mini skirt and a silver gray silk blouse with the top three buttons open. Her high-heeled shoes were gray and she wore a silver gray duster open over her outfit. She walked in slowly, looking at my office the way people look around at a museum. She stopped maybe two feet in front of my desk, holding her black alligator purse in front of her thighs with both hands. Her hair wasn't corn rowed today, it framed her head in soft black curls. She wore eye makeup and red lipstick, and probably more subtle stuff that I didn't know about. She looked maybe twenty years old and she was beautiful.

"I . . . " she started and stopped. She looked

back at the open door. "Can I close the door?" she said.

I came around the desk.

"I will," I said.

I went and shut the door and came back and pulled one of the client chairs a little closer to her.

"Sit down, please," I said.

She looked at the chair and then at the closed door. Her movements were all slow, as if she had to think through each one before she made it. She looked at me again and then at the chair and then carefully smoothed her skirt against the backs of her thighs with her left hand and sat down. She sat upright, forward in her chair, her knees together, both feet on the floor, side by side.

I went around my desk and sat down and smiled at her. Encouraging. Supportive. Attentive. Entirely without sexual or racial prejudice. She could tell me anything.

She did not smile back. She gazed at me without any affect at all that I could discern. She held her purse now in her lap with both hands.

We sat and looked at one another. The steam knocked for a moment in the pipes and then stopped. I heard heels clack in the corridor again.

"Dwayne don't know I'm here," she said.

Her quiet gaze didn't move. "He be really pissed off if he knew."

I nodded. Nice to hear a human voice again.

We were quiet some more. She turned the purse once in her lap so that the open end now faced her. Too bad I didn't smoke. The heels in the hall clacked back from wherever they had clacked before.

"Excuse me," Chantel said. "I don't mean to just stare like this, but I'm shy around white people until I know them."

I nodded again.

"I don't know many white people," she said. "Even at Taft I stay mostly with other black people."

"You live with Dwayne?"

"Yes, since the end of sophomore year."

"You going to get married, you think?"

"Un huh. After graduation. Dwayne probably going to be drafted by the Clippers so we probably going to move to LA."

"You mind?" I said.

"No," Chantel said. "Me and Dwayne be fine anywhere."

I nodded. "How's his reading coming?"

Chantel shrugged. We sat and looked quietly some more. She didn't seem to be uncomfortable with the silence. I wasn't either. I'd heard too many silences to get uncomfortable.

125

"You told anybody?" Chantel said.

"About Dwayne can't read? No, nobody that you'd care about."

"How 'bout the other thing?"

"Same answer," I said.

Chantel nodded, as much to herself as to me. I waited.

"You married?" Chantel said.

"Not quite," I said.

"You got somebody?"

"Yes."

She nodded again, as if I'd passed some kind of test.

"What you going to do?" she said.

"I can't seem to help Dwayne from Dwayne's end," I said. "So I'm going to try to go back door. I'm going to bust his connection and see if I can spring him free."

"Dwayne's a boy," she said. "I know we not supposed to say 'boy.' We supposed to talk that man child shit; but it's true. He looks like a man, and he's good as any man, but he hasn't grown up at all."

"He's been a star so long he's never had a chance to," I said.

Chantel nodded her head four or five times rapidly. "Yes," she said, "that's right, and he always been bigger and stronger than everybody and he never had to, you know, do stuff he didn't like, do stuff he wasn't too good at."

"Like reading and writing," I said.

"That's right," Chantel said. "He wasn't so good at that so he just didn't do it. He so good at other stuff that he don't have to do it."

"What happens when you try to teach him?" I said.

"He get mad," Chantel said. "No, he don't get mad. That's not right." Chantel paused for a moment and looked out my window while she thought. She pushed her lower lip. And frowned just slightly. I wanted to pick her up and kiss her on the forehead.

"He gets embarrassed," she said.

"Yeah," I said.

"He is very proud," Chantel said. "He got this whole Dwayne Woodcock thing he got to live up to and protect and be, and it cost him a whole lot to do that all the time."

"You grow up with him, Chantel?"

She shook her head. "No, he from Brooklyn; I grew up in Germantown. You know, Philly. Met him here, freshman year."

"Damn lucky thing for him that you did," I said.

"Why you say that?" Chantel said.

"Because you are a woman and a half, Chantel. What's your last name?"

"deRosier," she said. "Chantel deRosier."

"What would you like me to do, Chantel?"

Her gaze was steady and unembarrassed on my face.

"I want you to help us," she said.

"Chantel, I will help you do anything you want forever," I said. "Where would you like me to start?"

She shook her head. "They are bad people he's with," she said. "They don't care about him. They call him 'big guy' and they tell him how terrific he is and they pretend to be scared of him cause he's so big and so good. But they aren't scared. And they don't think he's a man like them. They think they've got this here poor nigger boy by the nose."

Chantel's eyes were shiny, maybe a little damp.

"And they have," I said.

She nodded. "Yeah, they have, and he doesn't know it. He think they the cat's ass. They got cars, they got money, they take us to restaurants and clubs, and give us clothes."

"They treat you good?" I said.

"They treat me like I'm Dwayne's piece of ass," she said softly. "And Dwayne don't seem to notice."

I stood up from my chair and turned and looked out the window for a moment, down at Boylston Street and the people moving by. I looked across at the trees in very early flower outside the building that used to be Bonwit's and was going to be Louis'. Right below me a young man in a tuxedo passed carrying a cluster of balloons that read HAPPY BIRTHDAY KATIE KROCK. He crossed Boylston with the balloons and headed on down Berkeley toward the river.

I turned back around and looked at Chantel. She was crying, though not very much.

I said, "Whatever comes out of this, Chantel, I'm going to do three things. I'm going to save Dwayne's ass, I am going to see to it that no one involved will treat you like anyone's piece of anything, and I'm going to make the bastards wish they hadn't treated you like that to start with."

"I'm not, you know," she said.

"Dwayne's piece of ass?"

"Yeah. He loves me. I love him. We got each other. We got a space nobody can come in. When we sleep together that's making love, it's not no piece of ass thing."

"I know," I said.

"How you know that?" Chantel said.

"Because that's the kind of woman you are," I said.

She nodded, the movement of her head barely perceptible.

"How you going to save him?" she said.

"Like I said, I'm going to go after Bobby Deegan."

"You get them it going to get Dwayne in trouble."

"I know, that's the part I haven't figured out yet," I said. "Be nice to get some feedback from Dwayne."

Chantel shrugged and looked at her lap.

"How much they paying him?" I said.

"I don't know. Dwayne never talks about that."

"Who's in on it with him?"

"On the team?"

"Yeah."

Chantel looked down and shook her head again.

"Don't know, or won't say?"

"Won't," Chantel said.

I nodded. "Okay," I said. "We figure it's Danny Davis."

Chantel didn't move.

"You know anything that will help?"

"Mr. Deegan got a friend named Gerry," she said.

"Gerry Broz?"

"Don't know his last name. White guy, scraggly mustache. Kinda fat . . . not really fat, just sort of flabby-looking."

"That's Gerry," I said. "You know what he's got to do with this?"

"No," Chantel said. "I just see them together when we go out. They talk to Dwayne.

Dwayne don't want me talking to them. He knows I don't like them. He's afraid I'll say something bad."

"Dwayne likes them?" I said.

"He likes Mr. Deegan," she said. "I don't think he likes Gerry so much."

"Most people don't," I said.

"Dwayne don't like white people exactly, but he likes them to like him, you know? He needs to have them think he's a big man."

"And Deegan makes him feel good?"

Chantel leaned a little forward toward me.

"Yes. Mr. Deegan got money, and he acts like he got money. He know what to do in restaurants and how to talk to headwaiters and what to tip the hat check girl, you know, that kind of man. Real sure of himself. Confident, seems nice, but very aggressive too, like a big success."

"Dwayne likes that?" I said.

"Dwayne been a star most of his life but he been poor most of his life too and where he lived was all black people like where I lived. But his was poorer. We weren't poor. And you'd see all these cool white guys on TV, and you didn't really think about it, and if you did you wouldn't admit it, but being a success got kind of mixed up with being white, or being like a white person, or having white people like you. Mr. Deegan is what Dwayne thinks he ought to be."

"He is better than that, Chantel, or you wouldn't love him."

"He needs to know he better than that," Chantel said. "He got to see that Mr. Deegan is a sleaze with nice manners."

"Okay," I said. "I think I've got it. I show Dwayne that Deegan's a sleaze, prove to Dwayne that he himself is not a sleaze, get Deegan off his back, keep anyone from finding out he shaved points, teach him to read and write and not let anyone know that he can't."

For the first time since I'd seen her, Chantel smiled.

"Yes," she said, "that's exactly it."

"And on the seventh day I'll rest," I said.

TWENTY

I got the call from Dwayne on my office phone at four thirty on a cold drizzly Thursday afternoon. Hawk was with me. We'd spent most of the last hour trying to figure out how to deal with the mess Dwayne was in, and we weren't making much progress. We were in the middle of a five-minute break devoted to a discussion of the paralegal's backside when the phone rang and I answered it.

"I need to see you," Dwayne said.

"How come?" I said.

"I been thinking 'bout what you said and I was wrong to get mad," Dwayne said. "I need to talk with you without anybody seeing me."

"I'll meet you," I said.

"Gotta be private, man. Nobody better see me."

"Wherever you want," I said.

"You know the parking garage by the Aquarium?" Dwayne said.

"Yes," I said. "On Milk Street."

"I be on the top level at six thirty," Dwayne said. "You come in your car and I'll get in."

"Six thirty," I said.

"Don't tell nobody," Dwayne said and hung up.

I said, "Dwayne wants me to meet him on the top level of the parking garage on Milk Street by the Aquarium."

"When?"

"Six thirty. Says he's changed his mind about me being a honkie motherfucker."

"He actually say that?" Hawk said.

"Well, he implied it," I said.

"Hm," Hawk said. "What you think?"

"Could be true," I said. "Or he could be doing what he's told and when I get there whoever Deegan hired instead of you will jump out of a Cutlass Supreme and shoot a hole in me."

"Wonder which it'll be," Hawk said.

"Me too," I said.

We talked a little and observed the paralegal one more time as she closed up for the evening. Then Hawk left and I put my feet up on my desk and my hands behind my head and closed my eyes and thought about things. At six I let my feet down, unfolded my hands

134

from behind my head and stood up. I had the Browning on my hip. I took it out, put it into the pocket of my leather trench coat, put the trench coat on and buttoned it up, turned the collar up, put on the tweed cap that Susan said made me look like Trevor Howard, and headed for the meeting with Dwayne, or whoever.

By six the rush hour traffic had congealed into jams on the Southeast Expressway and the tunnel and the Mystic River Bridge. At the turnpike tolls in Allston they were cursing one another. But in the city the streets were shiny with rain and almost empty. Later the people would come in from the suburbs for dinner, or to hang around Quincy Market with the collars turned up on their Lacoste shirts, but right now the city folks were having a couple of Manhattans before dinner, and I was driving from Back Bay to the waterfront in maybe five minutes, hitting the lights on Berkeley and at Leverett Circle and cruising along Atlantic Avenue by six fifteen. I was driving a black Cherokee that year, with tinted windows. I parked it across the street from the garage and sat looking through my tinted windows at the entrance. No point arriving early.

The rain along the waterfront was canted by the wind from the harbor and came in at about a sixty-degree angle against the windows on the driver's side. At the parking garage there was very little action. A car went in. Two came out. Guys with their ties loosened heading home late. Entry was an automatic gate and a ticket dispenser. At the exit was one attendant in her toll booth. At six twenty-nine I pulled across the street and took a ticket and drove into the garage. I wound up the rampways through the nearly empty garage to the top. There were seven or eight cars parked. I moved slowly down the empty aisle, the Browning out of my pocket now and on the seat beside me. At the end of the aisle in front of me a Ford station wagon backed out of its slot and blocked the way.

Not an Oldsmobile Cutlass after all.

I looked in the rearview mirror. A Chevy Blazer with body rot and a plow hitch had backed out and blocked the aisle behind me. I suspected that Dwayne wasn't driving either car. I was right. The people in the Ford got out of the side away from me and stood behind the car. Behind me another two guys got out of the Blazer. One of them had a shotgun. None of them was Dwayne.

Nobody did anything. I sat. They stood. I picked up the Browning from the seat beside me and waited.

One of the men in front of me yelled, "Spenser."

I lowered my side window. "Yeah."

"Step out and we'll talk." He had one of those plastic Red Sox caps that has an adjustable strap and plastic mesh in the back. The hat crown was too high, and the brim was too short, and he'd done nothing to break it in or shape it, so it sat on top of his head like a saucepan.

"I can hear you from here," I said.

"I wasn't giving you a choice, stupid," the guy with the cap said. "We got you penned in and there's four of us. Get out of the car."

"That's the ugliest baseball cap I've ever seen," I said.

He put his left hand up toward it, then caught himself and rubbed his face instead.

"Have it your way," he said.

He and his pal, a very fat guy with an untrimmed black beard, came around the Ford. Each had a handgun. Behind me the two from the Blazer began to move toward me. Behind them Hawk appeared and leaned over the hood of the Blazer and sighted down the barrel of a twelve gauge pump at their backs. The guys from the Blazer didn't see him, but the guys from the Ford in front of me did. I slid across the front seat and out the door on the passenger side of the Cherokee.

Blackbeard and the guy with the hat raised their handguns to fire at Hawk. The big boom of the shotgun came just as Blackbeard was slammed back against the Ford. Over the hood of my car I shot the guy in the baseball cap as he was shooting at Hawk and turned and stepped to the back of the Cherokee before he hit the ground and held my gun steady on the two guys from the Blazer that Hawk had trained his shotgun on from behind. Everyone froze.

In real time the whole sequence had probably taken ten seconds. In the slow motion of crisis time it had unreeled in ponderous elegance, and the crystalline immobility that followed was intensified by the lingering smell of gunfire, like an olfactory echo of the big bang.

"The set up got set up," I said.

Neither man moved.

"We can drill you," I said.

They knew that. The guns were their protection, but if they used them they were dead. They knew that too.

Behind them Hawk said softly, "Put them down."

They still hesitated, but only for a moment. The guy with the shotgun bent over carefully and placed it on the ground. The other guy, just as carefully, put the big .44 Mag he'd been carrying on the ground beside the shotgun.

"Put your hands on the roof of the Blazer," I said. "Back away. Spread the legs. I bet you've done this before."

They did as I told them. Then I went to the front of the Cherokee and examined the two guys we'd shot. They were both dead. I walked back over to the quick and patted them down. The guy who'd carried the shotgun had a .25 automatic in the pocket of his leather jacket. I took it. When I stepped away, Hawk came around the Blazer, the shotgun resting butt forward, trigger guard up on his shoulder.

"They picked a good place," Hawk said.

"Yeah. Two gunshots and nothing happens. No cops. No sirens in the distance. One of you guys pick this place?" I said to the two on the Blazer. The one in the leather jacket said, "No. Frankie did." He made a small head gesture toward the two dead men.

I said, "You can get off the car now." The two men shuffled their feet in from the spread and stood straight and turned around.

"Let's discuss motivation," I said.

The guy in the leather jacket had a Miami Vice two-day growth of stubble. The other guy was dressed against the weather in one of those oversized short jackets with lots of lapels and collars and cuffs and epaulets and doodads. The zipper was diagonal across the front.

"Whaddya mean?" he said.

"Why did you try to kill me?" I said.

"We was just going to talk with you," he said.

"What about?"

The guy in the leather jacket said, "We was told to talk to you about staying away from Dwayne Woodcock."

"Who told you?" I said.

He looked at the ground. The guy in the fancy jacket looked at him.

Hawk said, "We already dumped two of you. You think we going to have a lot of trouble going four for four?"

Fancy jacket shook his head.

"Guy from New York hired us, give us five grand, said to rough you up and tell you lay off Dwayne Woodcock. Said if you were stubborn, or we thought the warning wouldn't stick, we was to kill you. He left it up to us."

I looked at Hawk. "Twelve fifty apiece?"

He smiled and shook his head. "That's embarrassing," he said.

"It's humiliating," I said. I looked back at the two hoods.

"Twelve fifty?" I said.

The one in the leather jacket shrugged. He was still staring at the floor.

"Why not," he said.

"Why not?" I said. "For crissake, think

how I feel. Some guy thinks I'm only worth twelve fifty to whack? What kind of thing is that to learn about yourself."

Neither one said anything.

"Guy from New York named Deegan?" I said.

"He didn't say his name. He just gave us the money, told us what he wanted."

"How'd he find you?"

"Come into the bar where Frankie works, said he heard Frankie would do this kind of job."

"Worked," I said. "Frankie doen't work there anymore."

"So Frankie says, sure, and he gets the rest of us and we come to do this."

"Who told Dwayne to call me?" I said.

"I dunno," Leather Jacket said. "Frankie just said you'd show up here around six-thirty. Said the New York guy told him."

I nodded. "Okay, beat it. You run into the New York guy tell him he needs to hire better than twelve fifty apiece."

"We didn't know he'd be here," the guy in the fancy jacket said. He looked at Hawk.

"If I knew you were in this price range," I said, "I wouldn't have bothered to bring him."

I jerked my head toward the Blazer.

"Screw," I said.

The two of them turned and got into the Blazer and pulled away. Hawk walked to his Jaguar, parked at the near end of the floor. He opened the trunk, put the shotgun in, closed the trunk, got into the car and backed out. He lowered his window.

"Thanks," I said.

"Twelve fifty," he said, and shook his head happily.

Then the window went up silently and the Jag slid away down the ramp.

TWENTY-ONE

The next day I went to see Dwayne. I found him at the field house. He had no classes and he was there with three other players shooting around.

I stood in the shadows at the top of the stands and looked down at him for a while. Two of the managers were there, retrieving balls, keeping the ball racks full. There was some banter, some hoots at a particularly bodacious jam. Davis, the point guard, was the butt of a lot of teasing.

"Hey, white shadow," Kenny Green yelled, "you stuff one." He had a spare net he'd picked up and was holding it open at knee level. Davis went behind his back, drove toward the basket and pulled up for an eighteen-foot jumper, which he swished.

"Hit one of them, Kenny," Davis said.

Green, who had never played more than eight feet away from the basket, laughed and cut for the basket and Davis hit him with an alley oop and Green stuffed it.

Dwayne worked methodically around the perimeter shooting jump shots. One of the managers would pass him the ball and he would catch it and in the same motion go up for the shot. Every third or fourth time he'd fake the shot and drive. He did this without pause over and over again. He didn't do much talking, he seemed wholly focused on his workout.

I watched for maybe ten minutes and then moved on along the top aisle of the arena to Dixie's office. He was there. Tommy Christopher had told me that Dixie took Christmas morning off, unless there was a game.

"You got something?" he said.

"Nothing you'll like," I said.

"I haven't liked anything about you since you first walked in here," he said.

I sat in the chair across from him.

"Dwayne set me up last night to be shot," I said.

Dixie looked at me without any understanding.

"I mean he called me and arranged a meeting with me and when I showed up for it, there were four guys there and they tried to kill me."

Dixie shook his head slowly, persistently.

"Dwayne wasn't one of them?" Dixie said.

"No, but he arranged to have me there."

"He wouldn't do that," Dixie said.

"No, he just called and wanted to meet me in a parking garage and then decided not to come and, oddly enough, four guys happened to be there who want me to lay off this case and they had guns."

"Parking garage? There was a shooting last night at a parking garage on the waterfront."

I nodded.

"Jesus Christ," Dixie said, "was that you?"

I didn't answer.

"Jesus Christ," Dixie said again. "I . . . what are we going to do?"

"We're going to talk with Dwayne."

"Spenser, Dwayne's a good kid, he's a quality kid, he wouldn't . . . he must have been under pressure."

"We'll find out what kind of quality kid he is," I said. "So far he seems to me to be a loud-mouthed pain in the ass. I'm way out on a goddamned limb trying to save his neck."

"I know, I know, don't think I don't know that. But the kid is so great. We can't lose him. I mean he's a blow off the court some-times, I see him in the interviews talking about himself in the third person. I know he can be irritating. But on the court . . . Spenser, he is the most coachable kid I ever had. He's got better work habits than I have. He listens, he does what I tell him, he practices more than anybody on the team. He stuck with the program for four years. He could have gone pro after his sophomore year. But he stayed here out of loyalty, out of respect for me and his teammates. Guys with talent like Dwayne, they can dog it through college, take the big pro contract, never really learn the game. Dwayne could pass more, maybe, but he's got all the fundamentals. He knows the game. He feels it. Spenser, the kid is a genius in his own way."

"Get him in here, Dixie. I'm now covering up point shaving and accessory to attempted murder for him. I need to find a handle on this thing or I'm going down with him."

"You didn't report the attempt to the cops?"

"No," I said. "I couldn't figure out how to do that and not get Dwayne dragged into it. *What were you doing in the garage? Why did you agree to go there? Why did these guys want to hit you?* Cops aren't dumb. Cops been lied to a lot in their career. They know about that."

"And if they find out it was you and you didn't report it?"

"Pretty well eliminates my chances for the gumshoe hall of fame," I said. "Get him in here."

Dixie nodded. He rose and walked past me to his office door and stuck his head out.

"Vicki," he said to his secretary, "tell Dwayne I want to see him, please."

Dixie came back around his desk and sat heavily in his swivel chair.

"Goddamn," he said. "Goddamn."

We were quiet while we waited for Dwayne. When he came in he filled the room. It was always startling to see Dwayne up close. When I wasn't with him, I forgot how big he was and tended to think of him in normal-sized terms. But in shorts and a tank top, with a towel draped over his shoulders, he was startling in his size. And more startling in his athleticism. He moved as gracefully as any corner back, and he was built like a good middleweight boxer, except that he was six feet nine inches tall. As he moved the muscles bunched and rolled under his skin.

"What's happening, Coach?" Dwayne saw me but didn't look again.

"Come in, Dwayne, close the door, sit down."

Dwayne did all three and looked at Dunham. Dixie put his hands behind his head and laced the fingers. He leaned back against the spring on the swivel chair and took in a breath and let it out.

"Dwayne," he said, "you gotta help us."

147

Dwayne's eyes shifted to me when Dixie said *us* and shifted back to the coach. He nodded.

"Sure," he said.

"Dwayne, you got to tell us what the hell is going on."

"I don't know what you mean, Coach."

"Yeah, you do. You been shaving points. Last night you set this man up to be murdered."

Dwayne's head was shaking back and forth in denial all the time Dixie talked.

"You called him," Dixie said, "you told him to meet you in a parking garage, and instead of you, when he got there he found some people with guns."

Dwayne's head continued to shake.

"They weren't . . . He said they wasn't . . ."

"Who?" I said to Dwayne.

Dwayne shook his head some more.

"Goddamn it, Dwayne," Dixie said. "Think a bit. This man is trying to help you. I'm trying to help you. Now, goddamn it, how we going to help you if you won't tell us what's going on?"

Dwayne was still shaking his head. He wasn't looking at Dixie anymore. He was looking down.

"You got a responsibility, Dwayne," Dixie said.

Dwayne didn't raise his eyes. His head was still now, and he gazed steadfastly at the floor.

"Dwayne, you got a responsibility to this program, to me, to the other guys on the team."

Dwayne was motionless.

"You owe it to yourself, Dwayne."

Dwayne raised his head and looked at Dixie.

"I can't, Coach," he said.

"Why not?" Dixie said.

The connection between Dwayne and Dixie was real and concentrated. I got a hint of why he was a great coach.

"I got other responsibilities," Dwayne said.

"Responsibilities? Who the Christ to?" Dixie was outraged.

Dwayne shook his head.

"More important than the program, Dwayne?"

Dwayne looked at the ground again. We were all quiet. In the outer office we could hear Vicki typing. I watched the quartz clock on the wall for a while. The second hand jerked around the dial in one-second increments.

"Dwayne," Dixie said, "I'm going to have to sit you down."

Dwayne's head raised slowly until his eyes were on Dixie's face.

Their eyes held each other. I was entirely extraneous.

"You got to help us to help you, or I can't play you," Dixie said.

"Tournament startin'," Dwayne mumbled.

"Yeah," Dixie said.

Dwayne looked at him some more. Then slowly he stood up. He looked down at Dixie, for a full breath cycle.

"I got to go," he said.

"You change your mind, Dwayne, you know where I am," Dixie said.

Dwayne nodded and turned slowly away. He carefully didn't look at me. He opened the door and went out and closed it carefully behind him. The silence in the room was majestic. Dixie slammed his open hand flat on his desktop.

"Damn," he said.

"Yeah," I said.

We sat some more.

"What's your chances in the NCAA Tournament without him?" I said.

"Slim and none," Dixie said.

"What are you going to tell the press?" I said.

"Nothing," Dixie said.

"They'll be all over you," I said.

"Like ticks on a bird dog," Dixie said.

TWENTY-TWO

We were at my place. Susan was taking a bath and I was in bed reading Roger Angell's new book. It was ten o'clock on a Friday night. The door was locked, my gun was on the bed table, the television was playing with the sound off. All was peaceful. Susan came from the bathroom wearing a large blue towel and drying herself with it as she walked.

"Is there a wonderful movie we can watch on cable?" she said.

"No," I said. "I think we'll have to make love."

"And have a late supper after?"

"We had supper," I said.

"No, we had dinner," Susan said.

"Of course," I said.

"Well, if 'tis to be done," Susan said, "better it be done quickly."

She dropped her towel and dove onto the bed. I dog-eared the page and put the book on the bed table beside the gun.

Susan made her bubbly little laugh, which, in a less stately woman, might have been construed as a giggle. She pulled the covers part way back and wiggled in under them.

"Oh good," she said. "The sheets are clean."

She pressed against me.

"And," she said with her near-giggle lurking under the words, "I think you're glad to see me."

"You shrinks," I said, "you don't miss a thing."

"Some things are easier to miss than others," she said.

"I beg your pardon," I said, and she inched her body up a bit against mine and pressed her open mouth against mine.

All smiles ceased.

Susan's energy was limitless. She worked out every day, often twice a day. Her body was strong and very flexible. I was in pretty good shape myself.

When it was over we lay pressed together, our bodies wet with perspiration, our breaths coming in big heaves, our lips still touching. Susan's eyes were closed.

"I never remember how strong you are," Susan said with her lips touching mine as she spoke, and her eyes still closed.

"It's because my heart is pure," I said.

"Bullshit," she said.

"Good point," I said.

We lay like that for a bit, quietly. Then Susan rolled away from me and sat up without using her hands and got out of bed and walked across to the bedroom closet, where she kept a robe.

Eat your heart out, Paralegal.

She put on her robe of many colors and got one out for me. It was black, with a hood. I looked like Darth Vader in it. But Susan liked it. She draped it over the foot of the bed.

"What's for supper?" she said.

I put on my Darth Vader robe and went to the kitchen.

When Susan came out of the bathroom I was peeling an avocado.

"That looks encouraging," she said. She came and sat at the counter on a high stool with a fluted back. I put a glass before her and poured in some Cristal Champagne. She smiled.

"To us," she said. We both drank some.

"You have always had wonderful taste in champagne and women," she said.

"The taste in women is instinctual," I said. "I learned the champagne from Hawk."

I finished the avocado and sliced it over endive leaves. I added some mango slices and

153

put over it a dressing of first-press olive oil and lemon juice and honey. I put one plate in front of Susan and the other at my place and came around the counter.

Susan poured herself half a glass more of champagne and took a small bite of the avocado.

"Yum, yum," she said.

"It's only the beginning," I said.

"How is it going with Dwayne what's-his-name?" Susan said.

"Woodcock," I said. "It's going very badly."

Susan took a crescent of mango on her fork and dabbed it in the dressing and ate it in two small bites. Slowly.

"Tell me about it," she said when she was through chewing.

I did.

By the time I was through I had sliced some cob smoked turkey onto a plate with some tomato chutney. I checked the whole wheat biscuits in the oven.

"There needs to be a reason," Susan said. "Everything he cares about is pressing on him to act differently and yet he won't."

"I'm wondering, the kind of kid he is, is there some kind of jock ethic here?"

Susan clicked the rim of her champagne glass against her bottom teeth gently. I checked the biscuits again. They were golden. I took them out and put them on the counter to cool.

"Are you suggesting that he sees this gang of gamblers as his new team?" Susan said.

I shrugged. "Chantel says he thinks very highly of them. She says he needs white approval though he won't admit it, even to himself."

"Maybe why he's such a good player," Susan said. "Lot of white approval there."

"It helps that he's six feet nine and quicker than I."

"That quick . . . " Susan said. "Of course it helps. But there must be other people that tall and that quick who are not as good as Dwayne."

"I imagine."

"If so," Susan said, "won't Coach Dunham benching him change that?"

"Because Bobby Deegan and his outfit won't be so nice to Dwayne when he's riding the pines and can't help them shave points?" I said.

"Yes," Susan said.

I put the biscuits into a basket and put the platter of turkey and chutney on the counter. I got out some cranberry conserve that we had put up together last fall and set that next to the biscuits.

"I'm hoping for that," I said.

"But even if Dwayne turns against them finally," Susan said, "and tells you enough to put them out of business, how can you do it without exposing Dwayne?"

"I don't know," I said. "I was hoping if I drank enough champagne with you, I'd think of something."

"What you normally think of when you get drunk," Susan said, "will not do Dwayne any good at all."

"At least I'll be consistent," I said.

TWENTY-THREE

Susan went with me the next morning to Taft. It was a day when she didn't see patients, and she cancelled the class she taught at Tufts to join me.

"What is it exactly we're up to?" she said.

"We're going to look into the matter of Dwayne being a senior and unable to read," I said.

"And why are we doing that?"

"Because I don't know what else to do," I said. "Dwayne can't read and he's tied up in some kind of gambling scam. They're probably not connected, but since I don't know what to do about the gambling thing, I may as well look into the other thing."

Susan nodded.

"Better than doing nothing," I said.

Susan nodded again. "And where is Hawk?" she said.

"Around," I said.

"So how come I don't see him?"

"I don't know how he does that," I said. "But he can disappear if he needs to."

"But you know he's there," Susan said.

We were walking along a wide, hot, top path that curved up to the administration building.

"Yes."

"Because he said so?"

"Yes."

"And if those people try to kill you again and he's not there you're very likely dead."

"He's there," I said.

"Yes," Susan said.

We went up the wide granite steps and in through the Georgian entry of the administration building. There was a reception desk in the rotunda area and a long corridor that went straight through the building. We went past the desk and went halfway down the corridor and took some stairs to the left up to the second floor. Toward the back of the building on the second floor was Madelaine Roth's office.

Her door was open. She was at her desk talking on the phone. When she saw me she waved us in and gestured at the chairs in front of her desk.

"All right, Judy," she said. "Seven o'clock. Yes. Bye-bye."

She hung up and leaned forward over her desk and smiled at us.

"Dr. Roth," I said. "This is my, ah, associate, Dr. Silverman."

Madelaine stood and leaned across the desk and put her hand out. Susan half rose to take it. They shook hands and both sat down. Professional courtesy.

Madelaine sat back in her chair and put her palms together, making a steeple out of her fingers, and touched her lips with her fingertips. She said, "What is it today, Mr. Spenser."

"I'm still looking into the matter of Dwayne's illiteracy," I said.

She nodded, patiently, *this is my job, I have to put up with exasperating people.*

"How'd he get this far?" I said.

"I'm afraid I can't tell you," Madelaine said. "I am his academic adviser, but he has never been a student in a class with me. What strategies he employed to conceal the truth from us . . ." She turned her palms up and shrugged.

"What were his SATs like?"

"I don't really recall," Madelaine said. "It is, of course, confidential information."

I looked at Susan. "Confidential," I said.

"Isn't it always?"

I looked at the three degrees on the wall. B.A., Georgetown. M.A., Ph.D., Queens College, New York.

"Do you have Dwayne's class schedule for this year, and previous ones?" I said.

"Of course," Madelaine said.

"May I see the schedules?"

"What on earth for?"

"I am still looking for an answer. I am not getting anywhere with you. I thought I'd talk with his teachers."

"With his teachers?"

"Yeah."

"You can't do that," Madelaine said.

"Confidential?" Susan said.

"No, but, I mean you can't just walk around the University asking all Dwayne's teachers about why he can't read."

"Why not?" I said.

"Well, I mean, you'd have to make appointments, and, well, they wouldn't . . . many of them wouldn't like it."

"Would they not wish to reach an understanding?" Susan said, "as to how a young man who can neither read nor write could get a passing grade in their courses?"

"Do you teach, Dr. Silverman?"

"I give a course at Tufts. Primarily I am in private practice as a psychotherapist."

"Well, with a Ph.D. you've certainly been in an academic setting long enough to know, with your teaching experience at Tufts also, how prickly the academic world can be about any threat, real or imagined, to academic freedom," Madelaine said.

Susan smiled. "What greater threat is there to academic freedom than illiteracy? To any kind of freedom?"

"You will offend a great many people," Madelaine said.

Susan smiled more widely. "My colleague will weather that, I think."

We all sat for a few moments.

Finally I said, "Do we get the schedules?"

Madelaine shook her head. "I'm sorry, I'm just not comfortable giving them to you."

"Well," I said, "at least you have a good reason."

I stood. Dr. Silverman stood. Dr. Roth did not.

"Wasn't it Dr. Johnson," I said, "who called academic freedom the last refuge of scoundrels?"

Dr. Roth said nothing. Dr. Silverman and I left.

We walked down the corridor and back down the stairs.

"Dr. Johnson said 'patriotism is the last refuge of a scoundrel,'" Susan said.

"I know, but does Dr. Roth know?" I said.

"Unlikely," Susan said.

President Cort's office was in the other wing of the administration building.

"I warn you," I said to Susan, "this woman is infatuated with me. So be prepared to smother your jealousy."

Susan yawned. "I'll do what I can," she said. We went into the President's office and June Merriman at her desk looked at me passionately.

"Oh, God," she said.

"This will be hard," Dr. Silverman murmured.

"June," I said. "This is my friend Susan Silverman."

Ms. Merriman smiled with her lips only and made a small nod of her head.

"We'll need a list of Dwayne Woodcock's teachers, June."

"May I ask why?" June said.

"June," I said. "I know you want to string this out so you may spend more precious minutes with me. But Dr. Silverman here is my honeybunch and she's alert to even the most subtle of love ploys."

"Please do not be offensive," she said.

"Oh, June," I said. "How transparent."

"You won't leave without the list, will you," she said.

"No," I said.

"I can call the registrar and have Dwayne's schedule over the past four years Xeroxed. You'll have to make the list yourself."

She then made her phone call, prefacing the request with the phrase, "President Cort wonders if you would . . . "

In an hour we were having a spot of lunch at the Lancaster Tap. In a manila envelope on the table beside my water glass were copies of Dwayne's classes over the past four years.

"And what are you going to do with all those class schedules?" Susan said.

"I'm going to talk to all his teachers."

Susan shook her head. "You are a piece of work," she said.

"Says so," I said, "on ladies' room walls all over the country."

"No," Susan said. "It doesn't."

TWENTY-FOUR

For the next week I interviewed professors. Susan came with me when she could on the assumption that she was more academic than I was and could add some insight. George Lyman Kittredge couldn't have added enough insight.

I was alone when I talked with J. Taylor Hack, Francis Calvert Dolbear Professor of American Civilization. Hack was tall and portly and well tailored except that his shoes weren't shined.

"Woodcock," he said. "No, I'm afraid I can't remember the boy."

"Took your course in The Frontier Hypothesis, last spring," I said.

Hack smiled graciously. "It's quite a popular course," he said. He dipped his head modestly. "I'm just not able to recall all of my students."

"Gee," I said. "That's too bad. I thought

maybe because Dwayne is six feet nine inches tall and the best college basketball player in the world, you might have noticed him more than others."

"The best, really, how interesting. I don't pay much attention to basketball, I fear."

I was looking at my notes. "Dwayne got a B – in your course."

"Well, he did very well. It's rather a demanding course and for a, ah, basketball player to do that well, Dwayne must be an unusual young man."

"He can't read," I said.

"I beg your pardon."

"He can't read."

Hack was absolutely silent.

"Probably gotten an A," I said, "if he could read."

"It's not possible. Someone must have taken the exams for him," Hack said finally.

"Probably," I said. "And probably wrote his papers for him. You wouldn't have known if someone sat in for him during class?"

Hack paused a long time before he answered. Finally he said, "No, I wouldn't . . . there are forty or fifty people in this class, I give it every semester. I have two other classes each year. There're papers, and my own research."

"Anyone ever ask you to give his grades any

special attention?" I said.

"No. Good God, no. No one would intrude on the grading process like that."

"Of course not," I said. "And you never heard of Dwayne Woodcock?"

"No."

"Amazing," I said.

"I do not," Hack said, "spend my time poring over the sports pages."

"I know who Frederick Jackson Turner is," I said.

"I don't see the relevance."

"There's a surprise," I said.

Susan was with me when we talked to a young assistant professor named Mary Ann Hedrick. She had an office about the size of a confessional, in the humanities building.

"Sure, I remember Dwayne," she said. "I had him in the American lit survey, two years ago. Who could forget him?"

"He's easy to notice," I said.

Mary Ann winked at Susan. "I'll say," she said.

"Was he in regular attendance?" I said.

"In class? Hell no. He showed up once in a while and he'd come to conference in my office when it was scheduled. But he had practice, and then he had games, and it's hard for a kid. The course is required, and I'm sure was about things that he had no interest in. Imagine him reading Emily Dickinson?"

"He couldn't read," I said.

"Excuse me."

"He couldn't read Emily Dickinson. He can't read."

"What do you mean he can't read?" Mary Ann said.

"He's illiterate," Susan said.

"God, aren't they all," Mary Ann said. "But you mean really, don't you?"

"Yes."

"Jesus Christ," she said. "What is he now? A senior?"

"Yes."

"And he can't read," she shook her head. "Don't we look like a collection of prime jerks," she said.

"Yes," I said. "You do."

"We're interested in how that happened," Susan said.

"It happens because nobody gives a goddamn. Me included. The students are the necessary evil in the teaching profession. Otherwise it's a pretty good deal. You don't work hard, you have a lot of time off. The pay's not much, but nobody hassles you. You can read and write and publish, pretty well unimpeded except for the students. Most of us don't like them much."

"Anybody ever pressure you to give Dwayne a better grade or whatever?" I said.

"No," she said. "What did I give him?"

I consulted my list. "C + ," I said.

"And he can't read," she said. "Boy, is this embarrassing or what?"

"Dwayne's embarrassed too," Susan said.

"I don't give exams, and I don't take attendance. I give them two papers a semester, and I work on grading them. But I don't like bluebook knowledge and I don't like teaching kids who are there only because they're compelled."

"So someone wrote Dwayne's papers for him," Susan said.

"Sure," Mary Ann said. "I don't remember him now, but I probably suspected it when they came in sounding like an Oxford honors thesis, but frankly I figure you get more teaching done by keeping them in school than by flunking them out. Besides, the truth, charging him with plagiarism and flunking him is a pain in the ass. It's easier to let it go."

"Why is it a pain in the ass?" Susan said.

"They come in and whine to you and swear they did it, but their roommate helped them, and . . . " Mary Ann made a push-it-all-away gesture with both hands. "I'm doing a book on Ellen Glasgow, and I like to work on it when I'm not teaching."

"No pressure not to catch him plagiarizing?" I said.

"None," she said. "That's the truth. What are you going to do about this?"

"I don't know," I said.

"Will you tell people?" Mary Ann said.

"It's what Dwayne wanted to know," I said.

"We're all ashamed of this," Mary Ann said.

"That's the easy part," I said.

Now and then I'd see Hawk, drifting across the street behind me. Parking at the other end of the block when I got out of my car. Motionless and barely real at the far end of a corridor as I stepped into someone's office. He was there, for a moment, with the morning light behind him when I went to see Harold Wagner.

Wagner taught Black History and had given Dwayne a D in the fall semester.

"He didn't do much," Wagner said. "And he didn't seem very interested."

"Do you know that he can't read?" I said.

"I don't know it," Wagner said. "But I suspected it. He missed the midterm, and prevailed upon me to let him do a paper instead. He got an A on the paper. He said he was going to have to miss the final because of basketball. I said he'd have to make it up. I was skeptical

169

about the paper. He missed two scheduled make-ups. He said an incomplete would make him ineligible to play. That Coach Dunham was a martinet, not his phrase, about such things. I knew what was riding on his having a good senior year. I said he could take a D for the course. His grades in his other courses were such that a D wouldn't make him ineligible."

"And that was it?" I said.

"No. I spoke to Dr. Roth, the academic coordinator for basketball. I said Dwayne was academically troubled. That I questioned his basic skills and that I thought perhaps he should be tested to see if we could help him."

"What did she say?"

"She said she thought I was unduly worried. That Dwayne had been doing well in other classes, but that she'd talk with him."

"She didn't press you to alter his grades?" I said.

Wagner shook his head. I thought about it for a minute.

"I didn't want to take away his chance," Wagner said. "There's not that many of us get a chance like Dwayne."

"I know," I said. "I got the same problem . . . among others."

"It is Dwayne's fault too," Wagner said.

"Yes. He knows he can't read. He hasn't

done anything about it."

Wagner looked down at his hands for a moment. "Our fault too," he said.

"Yeah," I said. "It is."

TWENTY-FIVE

So far as I could tell no one had conspired to keep Dwayne in school, although Dr. Roth kept bothering me. If Wagner had told her, and he didn't seem to be lying, she had not only her own knowledge, but the testimony of a professor. Why would she run the risk of covering it up at that stage? For herself, the help-out-the-poor-little-darkie attitude might explain it. But once someone else knew, would she jeopardize herself? Not the Madelaine that I knew.

I swiveled my office chair around and pulled my phone closer and dialed information in Washington, D.C. In maybe two minutes I had tracked down the registrar's office at Georgetown University. They had no Madelaine Roth. I called the alumni office. They had a Madelaine Reilly who had married Simon Roth in 1984. She was a member of the class of '82. They did not know the status of the marriage; but Simon Roth lived currently in Fullerton, California, and Mrs. Roth lived in Newton, Massachusetts. I hung up and went to my file cabinet in the corner so when the door opened it was concealed. Susan said it was the single ugliest piece of furniture she had ever personally seen, though a friend of hers who worked for Bedford Travel claimed to have seen an uglier piece in Paraguay in 1981. I got out my file on Meade Alexander and thumbed through it. Ah ha! Gerry Broz graduated from Georgetown in 1983. So they could easily have been acquainted. Pays to do business with a professional detective.

While I was on a hot streak I called a New York City cop I'd met a couple of years ago when I had worked for Patricia Utley. He wasn't in. He'd call me back.

The office felt stuffy. I opened the window a crack and then went and opened my office door to get some cross ventilation. Hawk was leaning on the door jamb across the hall talking with the paralegal. I left the door open and went back and sat at my desk and thought about what I was doing. After about fifteen minutes of running it back and forth it was clear that I didn't know what I was doing. What I had accomplished so far was to make people want to kill me. I'd gotten Dwayne in trouble with his coach. I had already found out what I'd been hired to find out, and I wasn't telling the people who'd hired me. I knew Dwayne was shaving points. I knew Deegan and others had put him up to it. I knew Deegan was connected to Gerry Broz, and I knew that Dwayne's academic adviser could be connected to Gerry Broz. And I could find that out in time, if she was, or if she wasn't. And I knew that the faculty at Taft, by and large, didn't much care if Dwayne could read. What I didn't know was what good any of this did me, and how to get Dwayne out of the mess he was in without destroying his life.

I looked across the hall. Hawk had moved into the office and taken a seat next to the paralegal's desk. *Easy for him. All he had to do was follow me around and keep people from shooting me in the back.* I heard the paralegal laugh. *What's so goddamned funny? Probably be moving in with her Monday.* She laughed again, and the liquid hint of a giggle lurked in the laugh. *Probably wants me to be best man.*

The phone rang. I answered. A voice said, "This is Corsetti."

I said, "Remember me? The killing on Seventy-Seventh Street, guy named Rambeau?"

"Body'd been there about a week," Corsetti said.

"Yeah, that's it."

"What do you need," Corsetti said.

"I need to know about a guy named Bobby Deegan," I said. "Probably from Brooklyn."

"Why?"

I told him without naming any names but Deegan's.

"I don't know him," Corsetti said. "I'll check with Brooklyn and get back to you."

Across the hall Hawk's success continued.

In about forty-five minutes the phone rang. I answered.

"This is Detective Kevin Maguire," a voice said. "Detective Corsetti from Manhattan says you're looking for information on Bobby Deegan."

"I am."

"Okay. Deegan's been in twice. Once for grand theft auto when he was about nineteen. Once for hijacking a cigarette truck ten years later. He hasn't worked a day in his life. Been hustling since he got out of Queens College."

"Queens College?" I said.

"Yeah. Educated. Did a year of grad work there, too. Don't make no difference. He's a wiseguy. Grew up on the fringes of the Brooklyn mob. We can't prove it, but we're pretty sure he's one of the guys hit Joey Gallo."

"He married?"

"Yeah, lives in Far Rockaway, got a couple kids. But he fucks around. We're looking to

175

get him for a cash room stickup at an OTB parlor in Manhattan."

"Who's he run with?" I said.

"Got a pencil?" he said.

"Yeah."

"Okay," he said, "known associates," and read a list of maybe a dozen names. None of them meant anything to me.

"You know any connections he has in Boston?" I said.

"No."

"What else you got to say about him?" I said.

"Bad news," Maguire said. "Got sort of college manners, you know, a breezy yuppie. Guy's crazy. Keep talking to you nice and shoot you in midsentence. You'd never know he didn't like you."

"He does his own work?"

"Sometimes. Sometimes contracts out. Doesn't mind doing it himself. Mostly it's what's convenient."

"Tell me about the betting parlor," I said.

"Last December. Four guys, went in with a key after closing. Tied up a couple cashiers, got seven hundred thousand or so in cash, small bills, no serials. Everybody in Brooklyn knows it was Deegan and his outfit, but nobody can tie it to him."

"Had somebody inside," I said.

"Everybody figures that, but we don't have anyone for that either. We talked to both cashiers until they turned gray, they don't have nothing to say. Two dozen people could have got a key legitimately, two thousand could have scooped it and made a dupe. Things ain't buttoned up really tight over there."

"Nobody's flashing money," I said.

"Deegan's been flashing money all his life. Story is he's made some heavy scores betting sports."

"That's the connection up here," I said. "He's rigging basketball games."

"Point shaving?"

"Yes."

"Can you get him on it?" Maguire said.

"Well, yes and no."

"What the hell's that mean?"

"Means I probably can take him down on the point shaving deal, but not without taking down some people I don't want to take down."

"They're involved with Deegan," Maguire said, "they deserve to go down too."

"All you need out of this is Deegan," I said.

"Any way we can," Maguire said. "Any other name, too, on that list I gave you."

"Name Madelaine Roth or Madelaine Reilly mean anything to you?" I said.

"Not right off," Maguire said. "She got

something to do with Deegan?"

"I don't know. She was at Queens College, too, in grad school."

"Hey, there's a hot lead," Maguire said.

"She went to Georgetown same time as a local hood that Deegan's connected with."

"Jesus Christ," Maguire said. "You a campus cop?"

"She works at the school where the points are getting shaved."

Maguire was silent for a moment at the other end.

"Okay," he said. "I'll see if anybody knows her. Maybe she'll turn up on the computer. Goddamn thing must be good for something."

"Find something, let me know," I said.

"Yeah," Maguire said. "You too."

We hung up.

I observed Hawk's technique for a few moments, then I got out the phone book and looked up the paralegal's number and dialed. In a moment I heard the phone ring across the hall. She answered.

I said, "This is Spenser across the hall. There's an escaped sex fiend loose in the building. He's masquerading as a big good-looking black guy and I wondered if you'd seen him."

There was a pause.

"He's drawn obsessively to paralegals," I said.

"Does he rip off their clothes and do unspeakably kinky stuff?" she said.

"Often," I said.

"My God, he's here," she said.

"Want me to come over?"

"Hell no," she said. "Leave us alone."

She giggled again, blatantly now, into the phone.

"Oh hell," I said, "let me speak to him."

In a moment Hawk said, "Hello."

"I'm going down to Henry's and set new records on the Nautilus," I said. "If you're not at the moment of climax perhaps you'd care to stroll along and learn something."

I heard Hawk speak off the phone. "He worried," Hawk said, "that we at the moment of climax."

I hung up and headed out to the gym. The sex fiend joined me in the hall. "Jealousy an ugly thing," he said.

179

TWENTY-SIX

Without Dwayne, Taft won the Big East with an overtime at the buzzer victory over Syracuse and headed into the NCAA Tournament. Dwayne dressed for every game and sat on the end of the bench farthest from Dixie. The question was on the cover of *Sports Illustrated*, and the talk shows rang with it. Why isn't Dwayne Woodcock playing? Dwayne wasn't saying and neither was Dixie Dunham. The pro teams, Dixie said, were on his case worse than the press. Was there a reason that Dwayne shouldn't be drafted? Did he have a drug problem? Was there an injury? Taft's chances of getting to the final four without Dwayne were worse than my chances had been that day I fought Walcott.

Every day Dwayne showed up for practice. Every day he worked as hard as he always did. Nights he stayed in his condo with Chantel.

Hawk and I had taken to trailing along behind him.

"Figure now that he ain't playing and can't help them," Hawk said, "might occur to them that he can hurt them."

"So we watch his back to protect him from people that you're watching my back to protect me from," I said.

"You get into weird shit," Hawk said.

We followed Dwayne around for most of that week when I saw Dixie after practice.

"Cort wants to see you," Dixie said. "Says if I see you to tell you to get on up to his office now."

"Gulp," I said.

Dixie kept on walking toward the locker room. Dwayne passed me without looking at me and went into the locker room behind Dixie. I left Hawk watching Dwayne and walked up across campus toward the President's office. I was aware that Hawk wasn't behind me and I could feel the muscles bunch in my shoulders as I walked across the unsheltered quadrangle.

In the outer office of President Cort, June Merriman looked pleased when I came in.

"Well, where have you been? President Cort has been trying to reach you for two days."

"Mostly I was home," I said, "playing with

my knuckle knife collection."

"I'll tell the President you're here," she said. "Mr. Morton is with him! And Mr. Haller!"

"Wait, let me catch my breath," I said.

June pressed the intercom like someone lining up three cherries on a slot machine. "Mr. Spenser has arrived," she said.

I couldn't hear the response, but she could and she said, "They'll see you right now," and stood and walked to the door to Cort's office and ushered me in, gladly.

Cort was at his desk looking serious. Morton was standing at the window gazing down at the campus. Haller was sitting on a couch against the wall with his feet on the coffee table. He looked amused.

Cort looked up at me for a long silent moment. Morton turned from the window frowning. I bore it stoutly.

"I'd like a full report, please," Cort said. He had on a double breasted gray pinstripe suit and a large silk foulard tie.

"I haven't found out anything," I said.

"That's your idea of a full report?"

"Often," I said, "I'm referred to as the great compressionist."

Haller recrossed his legs on the coffee table.

"You've practically pillaged our student personnel records. You badgered a large

182

number of faculty members, Dwayne Woodcock is now on the bench, Taft is likely to
lose the NCAA championship tournament.
Neither Dwayne nor Coach Dunham will
comment on this. The national press is in full
cry." Cort's voice was a masterful example of
emotion under firm control.

"Aw, hell," I said, "it wasn't much."

"You have charged that Dwayne cannot
read," Cort said.

I didn't say anything.

Morton had his arms folded across his
chest. He had on a dark blue pinstriped double breasted suit with a large maroon silk tie.

"And you have nothing to report?" he said.

"Hard to believe, isn't it," I said.

"Mr. Spenser," Cort said, "we have been
paying you to find out things that we want
found out, not to disrupt this campus and
annoy our faculty."

"No extra charge for that," I said. "It's a
professional courtesy."

"There's nothing funny about this, Spenser,"
Morton said. "We want an accounting."

"Don't blame you," I said, "but I'm not
going to give you one."

Morton looked at Haller. Cort looked at
Haller.

Cort said, "Vince, do we not have a viable
legal position here?"

Haller smiled. "Sure you do, Adrian. Everybody has a viable legal position everywhere in this great land, whatever that means. But in fact what you can do is fire him or accept his report. All other courses are, ah, counterproductive."

"Counterproductive," I said. "Vince, you been taking night courses?"

"Flippancy is no substitute for competence, Mr. Spenser," Cort said.

"That's too bad," I said. "I was hoping to get by on it."

Cort looked at Morton. Morton looked at Haller. Haller shrugged.

"You leave us no choice," Cort said. "I'm afraid we're going to have to terminate our arrangement as of now. We will honor your expenses through this afternoon until five."

"Call it even," I said.

I turned and started for the door.

Haller said, "Wait a minute, Spenser." He turned to Cort and Morton. "You think firing him will get him out of your hair. It won't. He's got hold of something's tail, I know him. He's not going to let go until he pulls it out of its hole and sees what it is."

"He will no longer be welcome on this campus," Cort said.

Haller laughed. "You think he cares? He isn't welcome most places. He doesn't give a

184

shit, Adrian, whether he's welcome or he isn't." Haller turned toward me. "Do you," he said.

I smiled enigmatically.

"What have you got, Spenser?"

I shook my head. "I don't quite know, Vince. No, that's not it. I do know. What I don't know is what the hell to do with it."

"And you won't talk about it," Haller said.

"No."

Haller shrugged. "He won't let go," he said to Cort and Morton.

"We hired him on your recommendation, Vince."

"And you didn't listen to the warnings that went with it," Haller said. "He's good. There isn't anyone as good, let alone better. But he does what the hell he is going to do and if you don't like it he doesn't care. I told you that. You hire Spenser and sometimes you get more than you hoped for and sometimes you don't like it. You remember those words?"

Cort was angry. "Enough," he said. "If there was a mistake made, now is the time to rectify it. You're fired, Mr. Spenser, and you are to be removed from campus by the university police if you are in any way an impediment to the business of this campus."

"I love it when you're angry," I said. "Your whole face lights up."

185

TWENTY-SEVEN

When Hawk and I got back to my office there was a message on my machine.

"This is Maguire in New York. Nothing in the computer or anywhere else on Madelaine Roth. But Deegan has a girlfriend in the Boston area. Slips out on the old lady every other week or so and goes up there. You get anything, let me know."

Hawk and I looked at each other.

"Okay," I said. "That's more coincidence than I'm ready to buy."

"Be odd," Hawk said, "if it ain't Madelaine."

"So she knows Broz from Georgetown, she knows Deegan from Queens College. When Deegan is looking for someone to scrag me, she puts him in touch with Broz."

"Education a wonderful thing," Hawk said.

"She's got to be in on the fix with Dwayne," I said.

Hawk was quiet.

"So if I follow her around, after a while she'll lead me to Deegan."

"What you going to do when you find him?" Hawk said.

"Don't screw this up," I said. "It's almost a plan."

Hawk nodded.

"Okay," I said, "you stick with Dwayne during the day. I'll try to get the campus police to cover him at night."

"Thought they didn't like you over there."

"Why should they be different," I said. "I'll call Haller, and have him talk to the college."

"Be a good idea if you did that with everybody."

"Let Haller speak for me?" I said.

"In every instance," Hawk said.

I called Haller.

"Vince," I said, "there's some chance, I don't know how great, that someone might try to kill Dwayne."

"He is caught up in something, isn't he?" Haller said.

"Hawk will cover him during the day, but he can't do it twenty-four hours. Can you get the campus cops to cover Dwayne when he's home?"

"Yes."

"Are they any good?" I said. "Like they have guns and stuff, don't they?"

"They're all right," Haller said. "It's a professional force."

"Get them to cover his house," I said, "from six at night to seven . . . " Hawk frowned at me, ". . . ah, make it eight, in the morning. Hawk will take him the rest of the time."

We hung up.

"Seven A.M.?" Hawk said. "Surely you jest."

"Hell, I was worried you'd be insulted when I said you couldn't do twenty-four hours."

"*Can,*" Hawk said, "is different than *want to.*"

"Sure," I said. "See if you can keep him alive till the campus cops get there."

When Hawk was gone I called Frank Belson.

"I need the make and plate number of a car registered to Madelaine Roth," I said.

"And you think I'm a registry inspector," Belson said.

"I figure you wanted to be, but flunked the test," I said.

"Only way to flunk that one is to die near the beginning of it," Belson said. "How do you spell Madelaine?"

I told him.

"Call you back," he said, "unless there's a crime or something, and I get distracted."

He hung up. I sat and waited. In fifteen minutes Belson called back.

"1988 Saab 900, silver gray, Mass. vanity plate says MAD," Belson said. "Anything else I can do for you before I go back to crime busting?"

"No," I said, "that's fine. I'll remember you at Christmas."

Belson hung up. I went down to get my car and drive to Taft.

TWENTY-EIGHT

I got back to Taft around three in the afternoon and began cruising the faculty and staff parking lot near the administration building. It didn't take long. I found the silver Saab with the MAD license plate in the second row three cars in, right behind the administrative building. There was a green triangular parking sticker on the right window near the door edge.

I parked my car in sight of the parking area in an area marked *Visitors* and waited. It was not a complicated intellectual process and I was able to handle it. The campus police did not open fire on me. A cruiser moved by me once and the cop looked at me with neither interest nor recognition. At 4:37 Madelaine came out of the administrative building wearing a full pleated skirt in sort of a pale violet plaid, high lavender boots, and a gray trench coat with the collar up and the belt knotted rather than buckled. She carried a big straw bag and a smaller purse of gray leather and she walked very briskly.

When she pulled out of the parking lot I cruised along behind her. We drove east, picked up Route 16 into Newton, turned left on Commonwealth and ended up at a series of condominium townhouses just up the road from the big Marriott where the Totem Pole used to be. I kept going past and watched her park and walk to her door. She went in. I U-turned 100 yards down and drove back and parked across the street in the parking lot of a complex of garden apartments where I could watch her door. Which I did until eleven forty-five and went home. She didn't come out, no one went in.

I did this for three nights, picking her up at work and following her home. One night she stopped at the Star Market in Newtonville, another night she stopped at a liquor store on the way home. That's all. She didn't see anyone or do anything. I figured that if she and Deegan were a matched pair sooner or later he'd come to her house or she'd go to his. I figured he wouldn't show up at the University, so that left my days free to sit around and think about becoming an abbot.

The fourth night was Friday, and I scored. I had been sitting in the apartment parking lot for maybe forty-five minutes when a cab pulled up and Deegan got out with an overnight bag in his hand. He went to the door and it opened and he stood for a moment with his arms wide and Madelaine came out and jumped against him and wrapped her legs around his waist. They kissed for a considerable time and then Deegan carried her into the house, still holding the overnight bag dangling kind of awkwardly from his left hand behind her back and slapping against her buttocks as Deegan walked. The door slammed shut behind them. Deegan had probably kicked it shut with his heel.

I speculated on what might happen next.

Whatever it was did not involve coming back out. At ten thirty I gave up and went home to bed. Deegan was going to stay the weekend. That seemed pretty clear. Probably had been back to New York to see his wife and count his money and, maybe, bring in a hitter from the Big Apple to deal with me. So I had access to him, I was pretty sure, for the next two days. If only it were pretty clear what I was going to do with him. It seemed time to consult with Susan and, perhaps, Hawk.

Susan was in pajamas when I arrived. But I wasn't fooled. Her hair wasn't up. She was waiting for me.

"Hey," she said, "how's it going?"

"Bobby Deegan just showed up at Madelaine's house and she ran over and jumped in his arms and wrapped her legs around his waist."

Susan smiled. Her face softened, "Hey, how's it going," she said.

"Yeah," I said. "We'd probably hurt ourselves doing that."

Susan went to the refrigerator and took out a low glass pitcher with a glass stirrer in it. It contained a pale chartreuse-colored fluid.

"Gimlets," she said.

"Gimlets?"

"Yes, I decided we ought to have something that was *our drink*," she said.

"And you chose gimlets?"

"Yes, the color is so lovely."

I nodded.

"And we only drink them with each other, and we keep our pitcher and our two gimlet glasses by themselves and we don't drink anything else out of them." Susan's eyes were bright.

"I'll get a matched set for my place too," I said.

"Yes," she said.

"That's very romantic," I said.

"I thought so," Susan said.

"Wouldn't it be just as easy to jump into

my arms and wrap your legs around my waist?"

Susan poured out a gimlet over ice and handed it to me.

"Drink the goddamn gimlet," she said.

"Right," I said, "it wouldn't be easier at all."

Susan leaned against me and I put my arms around her and one thing led to another and we left the gimlets half drunk on her kitchen counter.

Around midnight we were quiet. I lay on my back with my right arm outstretched. She had her head against my shoulder.

"Madelaine and Deegan are the keys to this," I said.

"Is that what we're going to do now? Talk about your case?"

I nodded.

"Then it must be they who prevent Dwayne from testifying," Susan said. "Unless you've missed a great deal, and you usually don't, there's no one else that could be."

"Yeah, but what have we got on him and how do I find out?"

"Without exposing Dwayne," she said.

"Sure, that's the goddamned kink in the rope. Otherwise I just give what I've got to Taft and let them take it to the D.A. and you and I can go to Chicago and have dinner at Le Perroquet."

"And a gimlet first?"

"The whole ball of wax," I said.

"Is that what we've been involved in to-night?" Susan said.

"Yes, tonight was the whole ball of wax," I said.

"And you call me romantic," Susan murmured.

"Shucks," I said.

We were quiet.

"Is there a way to bring them together?" Susan said.

"Dwayne, Madelaine and Deegan?" I said.

"Yes."

I shrugged. "Probably," I said, "though you've got to understand about Dwayne. If he's recalcitrant, it's heavy work."

"I know," Susan said, "I know. You've mentioned that he's big, but you and Hawk can probably reason with him."

"Say we get them together, what have we got then?"

Susan shook her head. "No way to know," she said. "Certainly no less than you've got right now."

"Very true," I said.

"And perhaps we'll have some insight into the relationship that we don't have now."

"We?"

"Yes," Susan said. "It's somewhat my line

of work. Perhaps I might be able to add a use-
ful observation."

"Perhaps you might," I said.

TWENTY-NINE

In the morning Susan called Chantel for me. I didn't want Dwayne to answer and recognize my voice and hang up.

"Chantel?" Susan said.

Pause.

"Mr. Spenser calling, just a moment."

We were still in bed and Susan handed the phone across her body to me.

"Chantel," I said.

Her voice was sleepy.

"What you want?"

"Can you talk?"

"Not much," she said.

"Okay, listen then."

"Un huh."

"I want Dwayne to see Bobby Deegan and Madelaine Roth at an address in Newton I'm going to give you."

"I don't understand that, Ma'am." The "Ma'am" must have been diversionary.

"I'll be there, and Hawk, and my friend Dr. Silverman, the woman who just spoke to you."

"Un huh."

"So you've got to get him there under whatever pretext. What's a good time today?"

"Today?" Chantel sounded confused.

"Yes. This morning would be good. In an hour, say."

"We ain't even up yet," Chantel said.

"We need to do this quickly, Chantel. Can you get him there?"

"Yes," she said. "Two hours."

"Okay," I gave her the address and hung up.

"Kid's okay," I said to Susan. "No argument, no maybe. Just yes."

"And Hawk will meet us there?" Susan said.

"He's there now," I said. "I called him before you were awake."

"You awoke from an evening of rapture thinking business?"

"First I thought about the rapture," I said.

Susan nodded. "Hawk will make sure that Madelaine and her boyfriend don't leave," Susan said.

"Yes."

"Wise," Susan said, "though it came rather hard upon the heels of rapture."

"I'll make breakfast," I said, "and you can start getting ready."

"If I start getting ready now, I won't be able to hurry."

"I know," I said.

"I like to be in a hurry," Susan said.

"Puzzling but true," I said. I got up and put on my Darth Vader robe. Susan slipped out of bed and walked naked toward the bathroom.

"Except when I take a bath," Susan said. "I like long slow baths."

"Among other things," I said. Susan looked at me the way she does, sort of sideways. She took her robe from a hanger in her closet and slipped it on. Susan was never naked except when there was occasion for it. She always looked a little relieved when she got into her robe.

I headed for the kitchen.

Susan and I had sweet potato pancakes and two cups of coffee each. Decaffeinated. No problem. I didn't miss real coffee at all. We cleaned up the dishes afterward and then Susan said, "My God, look at the time," and began to speed around her condo. I went into the bathroom and took a shower and came out and found a neutral corner in her bedroom and dressed and put my new Browning on my hip, slid past her into the living room and stayed out of the way until she was ready.

At nine fifteen we were on the Mass. Pike to Newton. We got off at West Newton and headed west on Washington to Commonwealth Ave. and west on Commonwealth to Madelaine's condo.

"I still say it would have been shorter," Susan was saying, "to go straight out to 128 and come back in."

"No hurry," I said. It was seventy-three degrees and sunny, an atypical late March day in Boston.

"Easy for you to say."

Hawk's Jag was parked in the apartment lot across the street from Madelaine's. I pulled in beside it and Hawk got out of his car and climbed in my back seat.

"They there," he said. "Deegan came out and took the paper off the front stoop about half hour ago."

"How are you, cutie," Susan said.

"Formidable," Hawk said.

Susan leaned back over the front seat, and Hawk leaned forward, and they kissed.

"The basketball star coming?" Hawk said.

"His girlfriend says she'll have him here at ten," I said.

"And when he get here, what is it we going to do, again?"

"We're going to bring him in and observe

his interaction with Madelaine Roth and Bobby Deegan," I said.

"Interaction," Hawk said.

"They must be the people Dwayne's loyal to," Susan said. "Maybe we can get some sense of how or why."

"Besides, I can't think of anything else to do," I said.

"Could put them both in the river," Hawk said.

"Come on," I said. "Up here the river's almost swimmable again. Aren't you opposed to pollution?"

"We've done it before," Hawk said.

"The reasons were better," I said, "than any we've got now."

Hawk shrugged and leaned back against the seat.

"There need to be some reasons, Hawk," Susan said.

"Worried about reasons all my life, I be a long time dead by now," Hawk said.

"Yes," Susan said, "that's probably true."

Hawk grinned in the back seat.

"Don't make much difference to me, sweet potato," he said. "Kill them, interact with them, tell them about God. Whatever works. Or make you happy."

"How sweet," Susan said.

"There's Dwayne and Chantel," I said.

Across the street a bright red Trans Am slowed in front of Madelaine's condo and then swung into the lot in front and into an empty parking space. Susan and Hawk and I got out of the car and crossed Commonwealth and joined them. Chantel was in the driver's seat. Dwayne, looking a bit cramped, was in the passenger seat.

The car windows were down. Dwayne looked out at me and turned toward his girlfriend.

"What's he doing here, Chantel?"

"He's going to help us," she said.

"I don't want to have nothing to do with him," Dwayne said. "Let's get out of here."

Chantel shook her head and took the keys and stepped out of the car.

"Goddamn it, Chantel," Dwayne said. "Get your ass in here and drive this thing away."

"He's going to help us," Chantel said.

"That honkie motherfucker?" Dwayne said. "He the one got me benched."

"Honkie motherfucker," Hawk said. "He does know you."

"He'll help us," Chantel said.

"He'll help shit. Dwayne say get in here and drive, you fucking well better listen to Dwayne."

Chantel threw the keys into the car. "You

want to go. You drive it away. This man going to help us, if you'd just let him, dope."

Dwayne's shoulders hunched, and his head sank. He seemed to shrink in on himself so that he looked like a huge black Richard Nixon, looking out under his eyebrows.

Chantel stepped around the car to the open window. "Okay," she said. "Okay." She patted Dwayne's face. "Okay. I'm not mad. I love you, and I want you to be helped."

Dwayne's head was hanging. He stared at the floorboards.

"You're not a dope, Dwayne. I just mad when I said that."

Dwayne nodded without looking up. "Let these people help us," Chantel said. "I trust them."

Dwayne nodded a little and slowly got out of the car and straightened up. He didn't say anything, but he looked at me with a blank implacable gaze that didn't seem to mean anything, though it was clearly not friendly.

"Wait here," I said to Chantel and Dwayne and Susan. Then I started for the front door and Hawk came with me.

He stood to one side of the door, and I stood to the other. Hawk's .44 Magnum was out, the long barrel resting lazily on his shoulder. I took the Browning off my hip. It looked sort of embarrassing next to the Mag. "Is that a siege weapon?" I said. Then I rang the bell. Nothing happened. I rang it again. Then I could hear footsteps and a female voice say something that was probably "I'm coming." The door opened and there was Madelaine in a blue-and-white striped tank top and white shorts and leather sandals. I put the barrel of the Browning up under Madelaine's chin and said softly, "Where's Deegan?"

Madelaine's face stiffened and she said very slowly, "What?"

I pushed her backward and Hawk came behind me.

"Where's Deegan," I said again, softly.

"Patio," Madelaine said. And looked toward the back of the house.

The hallway went straight back along the right wall of the condo. The rooms all opened off to the left and a stairway rose halfway down the hall.

Hawk and I moved Madelaine down the hall ahead of us, and when we had about reached the staircase she seemed to come out of shock. She hollered, "Bobby." Hawk held her arm and I reached the door at about the time it opened. Deegan came in frowning in a lavender polo shirt and acid-washed jeans with a section of the *Globe* in his hand, his forefinger keeping the place.

"Bobby," I said, "how's it going?"

The muzzle of the Browning was right in front of his left eye as it adjusted to the interior light.

"What's this?" Deegan said and then as he looked at me, "Spenser? What's with the gun?" He looked past me at Hawk, who was still with Madelaine. A slow recognition moved across his face. "Shit," he said.

Hawk smiled at him in a friendly way.

"Let's all go in the living room," I said. "There's folks I want you to talk with."

"So," Deegan said, "knock on the fucking door, you know? How come you got to bust in here waving a piece and scaring the shit out of Mad?"

"Just being safe," I said. "You did hire some people to ace me."

"Hey," Deegan said, and shrugged a New York shrug.

We went into the big white-painted living room. There was a fireplace at an angle across one corner, and some Scandinavian modern furniture in white pebbly material, and a big teak entertainment cabinet with TV and stereo and CD, and VCR, and maybe a hot tub.

Hawk stepped to the front door, and in a moment Susan and Chantel and Dwayne filed in. Madelaine said, "Dwayne?"

Deegan said nothing at all, but he looked at Dwayne. Susan leaned against the wall to the right of the door. Hawk leaned on the left door jamb, in the door. The Mag was back under his coat. I had put the Browning back on my hip. The only place Deegan could be carrying a piece would be in an ankle holster and Hawk or I would probably be able to spot him bending over and unlimbering. I went and leaned against the mantel of the fireplace.

"These are my friends Susan and Hawk," I said. "Hawk is the taller of the two."

"Better dancer, too," Hawk said.

Susan had already begun to concentrate. When she did, other things no longer impinged. She was watching Dwayne. Dwayne was looking at Deegan.

"I didn't know you was going to be here, Bobby," Dwayne said.

"No problem, Dwayne," Deegan said. "No problem."

I said, "Why, you are doubtless wondering, did I call this meeting."

No one said anything. Dwayne continued to watch Deegan.

I felt like Philo Vance.

"We are the components of a vexing problem," I said.

Peripherally I saw Hawk grin and say the word *vexing* silently.

"Usually the problem is you don't know what happened. Here I know what happened,

I don't know what to do about it."

Everyone was watching me now, except Susan, who was watching Dwayne, and Hawk, who was watching Deegan.

"I know that Deegan stuck up an OTB in New York and started investing the money in a gambling scheme that involved point spread control by Dwayne. I know that Madelaine was the intermediary in the deal. I know that when I got involved and Bobby needed a shooter to take me out of it Madelaine put him in touch with her old school chum Gerry Broz, who without knowing the shootee recommended Hawk."

"Why not send the very best," Hawk said in a radio announcer voice with no hint of ethnicity.

"Hawk, being my frequent associate, reported this plan to me and hung around with me thereafter to help me foil it."

"You can't prove any of this," Deegan said.

"Might be able to prove the solicitation of a shooter," I said, "but your point is well taken. So far we can't prove anything much unless Dwayne is willing to talk about you."

"Dwayne is not a squealer," Deegan said.

Dwayne nodded silently.

"Or we could probably get this proved if we turned it all over to the D.A., but that would sink Dwayne."

"And you don't want to do that," Deegan said.

"No."

Chantel said, "I didn't know you was a friend of Mr. Deegan's, Dr. Roth."

"You know that, Dwayne?" I said.

Dwayne looked at Deegan. He didn't answer me.

"Did you know that they met at Queens College while they were both in grad school?"

Dwayne didn't move.

"You know she picked you out to help him control the spread?"

Madelaine said, "You don't know any of that, it's simply supposition."

"You pick Dwayne out for any special reason, Bobby?" I said.

Dwayne was frowning, slightly. Deegan didn't answer me. He simply shook his head.

"Makes sense, I suppose, to find a star you can buy."

The room was quiet. I didn't know where I was going, I was just trying to keep it going. I knew Deegan wouldn't say anything. He didn't know I wasn't wearing a wire.

"What made you think Bobby could buy him, Madelaine?"

"I don't know what you're driving at," she said.

"You steered Bobby, you must have. How

does a Brooklyn wiseguy end up buying a Boston basketball player."

"I'm from Brooklyn," Dwayne said suddenly.

"Did you know Deegan before?" I said.

"No," Dwayne said.

I waited. No one else said anything.

"We from the same city," Dwayne said.

"That how you guys got together?" I said.

Dwayne looked back at Deegan. The arrogance and pizzazz were gone. Dwayne was scared and confused and trying to disappear in upon himself like a rabbit trapped in an open field.

"Didn't Dr. Roth introduce you?"

"You don't have to say a word, big guy," Deegan said. "These people got no right to be treating you and me like this. And they couldn't get away with it if they didn't have guns."

"Dwayne," Chantel said, "how you meet Mr. Deegan?"

Dwayne made a shushing sound with his hand at Chantel.

"You want to get up and walk out of here now, Mr. Deegan," Dwayne said, "you and Dr. Roth, I walk ahead of you. I don't give a fuck about these motherfuckers. Dwayne Woodcock want to leave, he leave and his friends go with him. You want, Mr. Deegan,

I take you both out of here."

I liked him better then. It was a moment much better than the ones in which he sat looking at the floor. But I didn't like the development. Hawk and I weren't going to shoot him and he'd be a handful otherwise, with Deegan thrown in, who didn't look like a day at the beach himself. I would have thought of something, but Chantel saved me from it.

"They aren't your friends, Dwayne. Mr. Spenser's your friend. These people going to throw you away when they through."

"Dwayne," Deegan said, "have I ever lied to you? Have I ever given it to you any way but straight? You get out I'm going to represent you. I'm going to get you a deal with the Knicks, like Willis Reed never had, like Ewing never had. You know that. I know that. These people don't know. They don't matter, buddy. We matter."

"Let's walk out of here, Mr. Deegan," Dwayne said. In the doorway Hawk was motionless. The prospect of stopping a six-foot-nine-inch, two-hundred-fifty-five pound guy without shooting him seemed to present him no perplexities. He leaned against the jamb, his body loose, his face blank except for the hint of distant amusement that he almost always showed.

Chantel moved in front of Dwayne and took hold of his shirt with both hands. Her face as she stood was nearly level with his as he sat.

"No," she said, and her voice was scraping out of her throat. "No. You walk out with him and it's over for you. He's a crook. The cops want him. He's not going to get you a deal with the Knicks. You stay with me, Dwayne. You do what I say."

Dwayne said, "Don't you grab me, Chantel."

"I will," she said. "I gonna hang onto you so you won't drown. I won't let you drown with these people."

Dwayne said, "Chantel."

Chantel shook her head doggedly. She still hung onto Dwayne's shirt. He took her wrists and gently tried to pull her hands away. She hung on tighter.

"He going to ruin you, Dwayne." Intensity made her voice rasp. "Ruin you."

Deegan said, "Dwayne, you shut that little fucker up."

Dwayne still had hold of Chantel's wrists.

"She ain't no little fucker," he said, softly, a little embarrassed.

"Well, she's your broad," Deegan said. "Keep her quiet."

"See," Chantel said. "See what I am? See

what he thinks of me? That what you think, Dwayne?"

Dwayne shook his head as if he had a bee in his ear.

"No," he said. Still soft, still a little embarrassed. "No, Chantel, you know I don't."

"He don't care about me. He don't care about you," Chantel said. "He just care about gambling and making money. He call her a little fucker?" Chantel tossed her chin at Madelaine who was sitting as far back in a white armless chair as the chair would let her.

"Dwayne," Deegan said, "you let her come between us and the dream is over. You understand? Now you shut her the fuck up, or someone else will have to."

The minute he said it Deegan knew it was a mistake. But it was out and he couldn't reel it back in. Dwayne's head came up and he looked at Deegan as if he were a sudden intrusion.

He said softly, "Let go, Chantel," and she did and he stood, his head nearly touching the ceiling. He looked down at Deegan. "Who gonna do that, Bobby?" he said.

"Hey, buddy," Deegan said, "I just mean we got to have quiet so we can talk. We can't have hysteria, you know?"

"Who gonna shut her up if I don't?" Dwayne said. There was no referring to himself in the third person now. No swagger; and there wasn't any petulance either, any sulky confusion. "You gonna do that, Bobby? You gonna have somebody do that, like you tried to do with this guy?" He jerked his head at me.

"Dwayne, cool it, big guy. You misunderstood me. Hey, if I offended Chantel, I'm sorry. Chantel. No harm intended, hon, none of us want to be talking out of turn."

"How long you been sleeping with her?" Dwayne said. He was looking at Madelaine, who managed to look frightened and embarrassed and angry and above it all at the same time. If I got a chance I would ask her how she did that.

"Hey, Dwayne, nice talk," Deegan said.

"How long, Bobby? You scoring her while she telling me that you be a good guy to meet cause you had important sports contacts in New York?"

"Dwayne," Deegan said. "You're talking yourself right into big trouble."

"What kind of trouble, Bobby?"

"The kind that will take you down too, Dwayne. Don't forget it. I go, you go."

"I been a stand up guy for you, Bobby," Dwayne said.

"Better keep it that way, Dwayne."

"No, I don't think so. I don't think you a

stand up guy for me, Bobby."

"I'm not going alone, Dwayne. What you think you're going to do? Tell everything you can think of about me and nobody'll notice that you've been shaving points. That you're on the fucking pad? Get sensible, kid. I go, you go."

"Guess we ain't as close as you said we was?" Dwayne said.

"Close enough to go down the shit chute together, buddy boy."

Dwayne took a long step and was directly in front of Deegan. Deegan tipped his head back to look up at him. "And don't think I'm scared of you, Jumbo. The bigger you are the better target you make."

Deegan stood up unhurriedly.

"I'm walking," he said.

From the doorway Hawk looked at me. Deegan stepped around Dwayne. Madelaine said, "Bobby?"

"You gonna shoot," Deegan said to me, "start now."

I shook my head.

"I got more than I hoped for already," I said.

Hawk stepped aside and Deegan walked out the door.

THIRTY

"Where you suppose he's going?" Hawk said.

"Probably down to the Marriott and sit in the lobby," I said.

"Embarrassing to stomp out and stand around outside on the street," Hawk said.

Madelaine was looking at us in her living room as if we didn't have tenure.

"You're in this, Madelaine," I said. "When Bobby goes you're going too."

She shook her head.

"Yes," I said. "You are the yenta in this thing. You knew Dwayne was a good prospect. He couldn't read. He needed money. He trusted you."

"I can read stuff," Dwayne said.

"You knew Bobby had money from knocking over that OTB parlor. You knew he was looking to do something with it, put it somewhere would give him a nice return, account for his affluence."

"I had nothing to do with that hold up," Madelaine said.

"But you knew it took place," I said.

"I . . ." She looked around the room and her eyes rested on Susan. "Can't you make him leave me alone?" she said.

"I can't make him do anything," Susan said. "It would be easiest if you told him."

"Genie's out of the bottle now, Mad," I said. "No corking it up. Sooner or later it's all going to get said."

She shook her head.

"You in this with Bobby, ain't you, Dr. Roth?" Dwayne said.

She kept shaking her head.

"Get out," she said. "Get out of my house."

I looked at Dwayne.

"You ready to tell me about it?"

He looked at Chantel and then at Madelaine. His eyes moved to Hawk and to Susan.

"I got to think," he said.

I started to speak. Out of Dwayne's view Susan shook her head. I stopped and then started again.

"Okay, Dwayne," I said.

Dwayne looked around the room again. Then he put his hand out and Chantel took it, and they left, walking past a motionless Hawk at the door.

Hawk looked at me. I nodded and he trailed

behind them. If Deegan had been a danger before, he'd be a lot worse now.

"Are you going to leave?" Madelaine said. Her voice came out in a breathy rush. "Are you going to get out?"

I looked at her for maybe seven seconds.

"Sure," I said, and we left.

In the car I said to Susan, "Time to let Dwayne rest a little?"

"Yes," she said. "He'll come around. But he's giving up a male authority figure and it's hard for him. He needs a little time to find a new one."

"Be better if he didn't need one," I said.

"He's what," Susan said, "twenty-one? twenty-two?"

"Okay," I said.

"I watched him as all that went on," Susan said. "He looked at Deegan or you all the time we were there. One or the other of you. He was continuously aware of both of you and of the way either of you reacted to anything."

We were headed down Commonwealth Ave., past the Marriott and the canoe rental landing toward 128 and the Mass. Pike interchange.

"Deegan made a mistake when he threatened Chantel," I said.

"Yes," Susan said, "he did. And that's an encouraging sign. That his need for the young woman is strong enough to offset his need for the male authority figure."

"Might be something a little more than need," I said.

Susan turned her startling Technicolor smile on me.

"Love?"

"Maybe," I said.

"If love is more than need," Susan said, "or obsession or other pathological manifestations."

"You babes are such flighty romantics," I said.

I was looping around the complicated cloverleaf at the junction of Routes 30, 128, and 90.

"Is it love that made you go this way?" Susan said. "Because I think it's shorter?"

"No. This is stubbornness. I wish to prove to you that it's longer."

I dropped thirty-five cents into the automatic toll hopper and headed in the turnpike extension toward Boston.

"Love is what makes me care whether you know which way is shorter," I said.

She put her hand lightly on my thigh. I dropped my right hand on top of it and drove with my left.

"Professionally," Susan said, "I'm not at all sure that love, as such, is not simply a complex of human impulses: need, identification, possessiveness, fear of loneliness, impulse to replicate the family from which you sprang, sexual desire, anger, the desire to punish, the desire to be punished."

I didn't say anything. The Cherokee had tinted glass and with the windows closed the interior was quiet and cool. There weren't many cars out on a Sunday midday in late March, and the hum of the car's passage was all there was for sound.

"On the other hand . . . " I said.

"On the other hand I love you so much I could swoon," Susan said.

"Swoon?"

"Swoon."

"And the fact that Dwayne feels swoonie over Chantel," I said, "means he's capable of forming healthier attachments than the one with Deegan."

"I only said I was swoonie over you," Susan said. "I can't speak for Dwayne or Chantel. But the rest of it is right."

"Chantel says he needs white approval," I said.

"Yes, so a white male authority figure may even be more important to him than it would be to some," Susan said.

"What do you recommend?"

"Let Chantel work on him," Susan said.

"Let him think about what's happened to him, and let him come to it himself. You don't want him to feel pushed or he's very likely to clam up and if you push him hard enough you can push him right back to Deegan. Deegan says things Dwayne likes to hear. You keep telling him unpleasant stuff."

"I keep telling him to grow up," I said.

"And that he's risking jail, and that he can't read, and that he should testify against a man who makes Dwayne feel like he's more important than oxygen," Susan said.

"Are you suggesting he doesn't enjoy that?"

"Only a suggestion," Susan said.

We went off at the Allston/Cambridge exit and wove through the silliest exit ever devised to Soldiers Field Road.

I looked at my watch. Susan glanced at hers and then turned to look out at the red brick Harvard buildings.

"Two minutes faster than my way," I said.

She turned and smiled at me a smile of infinite sweetness.

"Shut up," I said.

THIRTY-ONE

I was in Lt. Martin Quirk's office at Homicide. Quirk was there, and Frank Belson, and a young cop from Walford named Stuart Delaney, a former state cop named LeMaster, who was the Chief of the Taft U. police, and a guy from the Middlesex D.A.'s office named Arlett.

Quirk was sitting square in his chair behind his desk, his forearms resting on the desktop, his thick hands motionless on his blotter. Belson sat in a straight chair, tipped back against the wall to Quirk's left, smoking a cheap narrow cigar, with his hat on and tilted down over his forehead. The rest of us ranged in straight chairs in a semicircle facing Quirk. Quirk was looking at me.

"Why, you are perhaps asking yourself," Quirk said to me, "did Lt. Quirk invite me to his office at this time with these other gentlemen?"

"I assumed you were holding a crime stoppers seminar and wanted me to lecture," I said.

"Well, that's close," Quirk said. "Actually these gentlemen all wish to learn from you what the fuck is going on with Dwayne Woodcock?"

"So where do you come in?" I said.

"Because the Walford police asked me to pick you up and hold you for them, and I thought it might make more sense if we all got together and shared our thoughts on this matter."

"You're Homicide," I said.

Quirk looked at Belson. Belson looked up from under his hat brim.

"Man knows his cops, Marty," Belson said.

"Who's dead?" I said.

"We'll ask the questions," Arlett said to me, "if you don't mind."

I looked at Quirk. "We'll ask the questions?" I said.

Quirk shook his head.

"Kid named Danny Davis," Quirk said.

I felt a tickle of relief. It wasn't Dwayne.

"Lieutenant," Arlett said, "I'll conduct this interrogation."

Quirk looked at him for a moment. Nothing appeared to change in Quirk's face, but the room seemed very quiet. Then Quirk looked back at me.

"Somebody shot him behind the left ear outside the Taft field house," Quirk said, "and then shot him in the back of the head after he'd fallen and was lying face down. Big caliber gun, maybe .45 they tell me."

"And we know you know more than you're telling," Arlett said in a rush. I could see Belson smile slightly.

Quirk ignored Arlett. "And then," he said, "somebody apparently made a run at Woodcock, and your goomba, Hawk, ah, interceded."

"Shooter dead?" I said.

"Two of them," LeMaster said. "No I.D. on them. Delaney got prints and they're going to run it down for us at Ten-Ten."

"State Police Headquarters," Arlett said.

Belson's grin got a little wider.

"Gave us a statement," Delaney said, "and released Woodcock and the broad . . . "

"Chantel," I said.

"Yeah, Woodcock's broad."

I said, "She has a name. It's Chantel."

"Sure," Delaney said. "They support Hawk's statement that he acted in their defense."

"So what do you know about all of this?" Arlett said.

"Nothing," I said.

"Lieutenant, arrest him," Arlett said, "read

223

him his rights and book him."

"Suspicion of murder?" Quirk said.

"Material witness, obstructing justice, anything you want. I want him in a cell thinking about this. Maybe his memory will improve."

"Didn't Robert Stack say that, in 'The Untouchables'?" I said.

"You're not as funny as you think you are," Arlett said.

"Yeah, sure he did," I said. "He said it to Bruce Gordon, who was playing Frank Nitti, 'maybe your memory will improve,' he said. And . . ."

"Shut up," Arlett said.

"I bet you watched that all the time," I said. "I know it was Ness who said, 'we'll ask the questions.'"

"Spenser," Quirk said, "give it a rest."

"Farantino's got a bad caseload problem in Middlesex," Belson said, around his cigar. "Sends out the best he's got available."

Arlett turned toward Belson. "Sergeant, just what the hell is that supposed to mean?"

Belson's thin face with its permanent five o'clock shadow was sincere as he looked at Arlett.

"Trying to be supportive," he said.

Quirk stood up.

"You gentlemen wait here," he said. "Frank, Spenser, come with me."

He went around his desk and out the door of his office without waiting to see if we'd come.

We came. He went along through the squad room and out and down a corridor and in through a door marked OCU. It was another squad room, a little smaller than Homicide. We walked through toward a door that read SGT. MYLES HICKMAN, COMMANDER, and opened the door.

"Myles is on vacation," Quirk said.

He sat behind the desk and I sat in front and Belson closed the pebbly glass door and leaned on the wall beside it.

"Okay," Quirk said. "Arlett's an asshole, you know it, Frank knows it, I know it. He's new in the criminal division, he's insecure and he should be. So he tries to be tough and he don't know how. But the questions he's asking aren't questions that shouldn't be answered. And if he pushes me I'll have to arrest you for him. They'll hold you in Walford."

"For how long," I said.

"Until Haller gets there. If we bust you, I'll have Frank call him."

I got up and stood looking out at the nearly empty squad room. At the far end was a dark-haired cop with a thick mustache. His baseball jacket was hung on the back of his chair. He was wearing his gun in a shoulder holster and a set of handcuffs dangled as well from the strap under his arm. He had his feet up on the desk. He was wearing New Balance running shoes and jeans. He hunched his right shoulder up to hold the phone against his ear while he fumbled for something in the desk drawer.

"I should have had Davis covered too," I said.

The cop on the phone found a pad of yellow paper in the drawer and began to write on it with a ballpoint pen.

"And I simply didn't think of it," I said.

I turned and looked at Quirk and Belson.

"I didn't think of it."

"Too late now," Belson said.

I nodded.

"I know who had him killed, and I know who sponsored the run at Dwayne, and I know why, but I can't prove it."

"Give it to us," Quirk said. "Maybe we can prove it."

"Arlett's going to prove it?"

"They got some good people working out of there," Quirk said. "Stegman, Russo."

I nodded again.

"The other problem is I will have to implicate someone I don't want to implicate."

"Life's hard," Quirk said.

"Kid already knows that," I said. "I'm try-

226

ing to make it a little easier."

"Woodcock?"

"I'm not going to say."

"What are you trying to do?" Quirk said.

"I'm trying to figure out a way to nab the son of a bitch who had Davis killed, without nabbing the kid he corrupted."

"You want to do this legal?" Quirk said.

"Doesn't make too much difference," I said.

"I didn't figure it did," Quirk said.

"But the kid's got to learn some stuff out of this," I said.

"Father Flanagan," Belson murmured.

"So you don't just ace the bad guy and call it even," Quirk said.

"No," I said.

"Not like you wouldn't do it," Quirk said.

"Not this time, at least," I said.

"You want to tell me the bad guy's name?" Quirk said.

"Informally?" I said.

Quirk laughed a little short laugh with his mouth closed.

"You mean will I tell Arlett?" he said.

I nodded.

"No," Quirk said.

"Okay. Guy named Bobby Deegan. New York wants him for knocking over an OTB parlor. He's been fixing Taft basketball games and was using Woodcock and, apparently, the Davis kid to beat the spread."

"I heard Taft hired you on that," Quirk said.

"And fired you," Belson said.

"And I got in there and stirred things up, and got so close to Deegan that he tried to hit me, and failed."

"Parking garage on Milk Street?" Quirk said.

I shrugged.

"And then he realized that the only people could put him away were the people he'd bought," I said.

"So he had them hit," Quirk said. "Except you figured he'd try for Woodcock, so you had Hawk there."

"Days," I said. "Dumb bastards had waited an hour they'd have had the campus cops to deal with instead of Hawk."

"Be my choice," Belson said.

"So you sink Deegan, and he takes Dwayne down with him," Quirk said.

"If we can keep him alive," I said.

"He's too hot," Quirk said. "Be hard to get anyone to try for him now. I wouldn't take the guards away, but I think you got a little time."

I nodded.

"So what are you going to do?" Quirk said.

228

"I'll think of something," I said.

"Too bad you didn't think of it before they killed Davis," Quirk said.

"Yeah," I said.

THIRTY-TWO

We went back to Quirk's office and teased Arlett for a while and then LeMaster and Delaney took me back to Walford in cuffs and stuck me in the Walford jail as a material witness. I was in for about two and a half hours before Haller came down with a writ and got me out.

The prisons in the state were sleeping four to a cell, but the town jails were as empty and quiet as a church on Wednesday. I alternated my time while I sat on the bare bunk between thinking about women I'd slept with and reanalyzing my all-time all-star baseball team. In recent years I'd replaced Brooks Robinson with Mike Schmidt and Marty Marion with Ozzie Smith. Now and then I wondered how the hell I ended up in jail in a case when I knew what happened and who did it and could probably prove it. But mostly I thought about women and baseball.

When I got back to my office it was late afternoon and raining. I was wearing my leather jacket to keep my gun dry and I had my collar up when I walked in from the alley where I parked. When I got out of the elevator on the second floor the corridor had that gray look that indoors gets on days like this one, and the lights from open doors along the corridor made yellow splashes on the corridor floor. One of the open doors was mine. I unzipped my jacket before I went in.

Hawk was at my desk reading a book with his feet up. He was wearing lizard skin cowboy boots. He glanced at me over the book.

"Cops talk to you?" he said.

"Yeah," I said. "What are you reading?"

"Book by Stephen Hawking," Hawk said. " 'Bout the universe."

"Only that?" I said.

"Campus cops and Walford cops and some state cops all hanging around Dwayne," Hawk said. "Figured I wasn't needed."

"Tell me about the hit on Dwayne," I said.

"Two guys pull up about five, quarter of, park in front of the condo, walk up to Dwayne's place and ring the bell. Door opens and they go in quick. I figure I better go in right after them and I do. They in the living room with Dwayne and the girl."

"Chantel," I said.

"Un huh, and there's an Uzi showing, so I say 'How dee doo' and shoot the guy with the Uzi and his associate turn around with a hand gun and . . . " Hawk shrugged and made a shooting motion with the forefinger and thumb of his right hand, bringing the thumb down like a hammer falling.

"Chantel sort of moaning and got her face against Dwayne, and he hanging on to her like she gonna blow away, so I call the campus blue bellies and pretty soon there a lot of people there."

"Danny Davis got killed," I said. "They tell you that?"

"Yeah. Should a had him covered too," Hawk said.

"I know," I said.

"Can't think of everything," Hawk said.

"I'll say."

We looked at each other silently for a moment. Then Hawk nodded. I did too.

"What we going to do about this?" Hawk said.

"Dwayne will turn," I said.

"Better than dying," Hawk said.

"So we're going to have some leverage on Deegan," I said.

" 'Less Dwayne runs," Hawk said.

I looked at him.

"Think like Dwayne. You black, you look

232

up to white people, but you scared of them. You don't trust them. All your life they been calling you nigger, acting like you don't matter. Now, he got his life on the line, his girlfriend's life on the line. He can trust the system, trust the white cops and the white judge to protect him, same system been telling him he don't matter for the last twenty-one years. Stand up to a white guy wants to kill him and count on the white system to protect him."

"Or," I said, "he can run. He can bury himself in the black ghetto of choice and hide for the rest of his life."

"What would you do?" Hawk said.

"Run for the ghetto," I said.

Hawk nodded.

"Can you watch him," I said.

"Can't watch him forever," Hawk said. Then he smiled. "Well, I could, but I don't want to."

"Stay with him a couple of days, give me time to try and put something together."

"You want me to stop him if he runs?" Hawk said.

"No," I said. "Just want to know where he runs to."

Hawk went to hang around outside of Dwayne's, and I went to my desk and sat down and called Detective Maguire in Brooklyn.

Things were looking up; I got him.

"I'm going off duty, in fact I was supposed to go off a half hour ago," Maguire said.

"I thought you New York guys never slept," I said.

"We don't," Maguire said, "but we need time off for fucking. What do you want?"

I said, "If I got Deegan to turn on that OTB thing would you deal?"

"Maybe."

"If I got him to give you the rest of the outfit, can you get him immunity?"

"He turns on the rest of the outfit and he'll need witness protection. That's Feds."

"Will the federal attorney deal on this?"

"Ain't a federal crime," Maguire said. "Why's he give a shit?"

"That's up to you," I said, "convince him."

"Yeah?"

"Can you do that?" I said.

"Maybe."

"Why don't you look into it and find out," I said.

"How you going to get Deegan to turn?" Maguire said.

"That's my problem," I said. "You work on what he'll get if I do."

"Hey," Maguire said, "I gotta know you'll turn him. I'm not going to be walking around down here saying he's turned, and find out he hasn't, and end up looking like an asshole."

"Would anyone see the change?" I said.

"I mean it," Maguire said. "I'm not sticking my neck out on the word of some guy I never even met. I mean I talked to you twice on the phone, and you got me making deals with the federal attorney."

"Magic," I said, "isn't it."

"It's bullshit," Maguire said. "You gonna turn him or not?"

"I'll turn him," I said.

"You do and we'll talk," Maguire said. "We can work something out."

"Might get your picture in the *Daily News*," I said.

Maguire hung up without comment.

I swiveled around and looked at the rain washing down my window. Now I could discuss these things with Deegan. If I could find him. If he didn't shoot me when I did. If Dwayne would testify.

"I need a drink," I said out loud.

No one said no. So I sat in my chair, got out a bottle of Glenfiddich and a glass and poured some neat and sipped it and watched the rain as night settled in behind it.

THIRTY-THREE

I didn't have to find Bobby Deegan. He found me. I'd been sitting maybe an hour and a half watching it rain when he walked into my office without knocking. The only light in the room was my desk lamp with the Tiffany glass lamp shade that Susan had insisted would dress up the whole office. When I heard the door open, I swung around and opened the right hand drawer of the desk. I kept a spare gun in there and it was always nice to have it handy.

Deegan stood in the doorway with the light from the corridor behind him. He wore an oversized, lightweight trench coat with the collar up, and a gray tweed cap.

"I'm not here for trouble," Deegan said.

I waited.

"We need to talk," he said.

I nodded at the chair in front of my desk. He unbuttoned his coat and sat down and stuck his legs out straight in front of him. I took a second glass out of the left hand drawer and put it on the desk and poured some Glenfiddich into it. Deegan leaned forward and took the glass and sniffed it and took a sip. He swallowed, and nodded his head.

"Single malt," he said.

We were quiet, the rain blurring down outside the window behind me.

"You're trouble," Deegan said.

"Nice of you to notice."

"Can't seem to get you out of the fucking way," Deegan said.

I nodded. We both sipped some scotch. Sipped thoughtfully, an ounce and a quarter of Glenfiddich will last half an evening.

"So what are we going to do about this mess?" Deegan said.

"I been giving that some thought," I said.

"Those were good people went after Dwayne," Deegan said. "Brooklyn guys. Guy Dwayne's size, you want the best."

I waited. Deegan would get to where he was going.

"You do them?" he said.

I shook my head.

"Black guy?"

I nodded.

"Gerry said he was good," Deegan said.

He was holding the glass of scotch in both

hands in front of his chin, elbows resting on the arms of the chair. He rubbed his chin absently on the rim. I could hear the faint scratch of his beard against it. Deegan looked like a guy who would have to shave twice a day.

"Guys Gerry sent me for you didn't work out too good either," he said.

"Boston guys," I said.

Deegan nodded. He drank a little scotch. I pushed the bottle across the desk and he leaned forward and poured himself another inch, and pushed the bottle back across the desk to me. He leaned back in his chair again.

"I want out of this," he said.

"Un huh."

"I want to deal."

"What you got to deal with?" I said.

"I keep my trap shut about Dwayne," he said.

"And what do I do?"

"You walk," he said. "And I walk and nobody says nothing."

"And nobody shoots Dwayne?" I said.

"Nobody shoots him, nobody bribes him, nobody mentions his name again."

I leaned my head back against the padding on my chair. I was tired. Tired of Deegan, tired of Dwayne, tired of tough guys and cops and guns and deals. I was tired of almost everything but Susan.

"Whaddya think?" Deegan said.

I shook my head slowly, still against the back of my chair.

"No?" Deegan said. "Why no?"

"Davis," I said.

"Davis," Deegan said, "why do you give a fuck about Davis? You got nothing to do with Davis."

"Got to get something for Davis," I said.

Deegan took in a long breath and let it out and dipped his nose into the glass for a moment and swallowed.

"You got to get something for Davis," he said.

I nodded.

"How about getting dead for Davis?" Deegan said.

"Hard to do," I said.

Deegan nodded slowly. "Yeah," he said. "It is."

He drank again.

"But it's not impossible," he said.

"I can put you away on the gambling charge," I said. "Dwayne will testify. So will I. You're a known hoodlum. You'll be a long time gone."

The wind seemed to have shifted. I could hear the rain being driven at a slant against the window behind me.

"What do you want for Davis?" Deegan said.

"The rest of the OTB crew."

"OTB?"

"You and some other guys knocked over an Off Track Betting parlor in New York. I want the guys you did it with."

"I can't do that," Deegan said. "They'd fucking kill me."

"I'll get you a witness protection deal. You aren't prosecuted and the Feds will give you a new identity and relocate you."

"All to keep you from pushing this gambling thing?" he said.

"And I don't tell your wife about Madelaine," I said.

Deegan looked at me a long time without speaking.

"You are a hard fucking case," he said, "aren't you?"

The question was rhetorical. I didn't comment.

"For a fucking arrogant asshole kid, talks about himself in the third person," Deegan said.

"He's good at what he does," I said.

"So what the fuck is that to you?" Deegan said.

"Girlfriend's nice, too," I said.

"Chantel?"

"Yeah, she sees something in him."

"So what the fuck is *that* to you?" Deegan said.

"You want to deal, or not?" I said.

Deegan stood slowly, and put his whiskey glass on my desk and walked over to the wall to the right of my desk and stretched both hands above his head and leaned on the wall. He did a couple of push-aways on the wall and then turned and leaned his back against it.

"Who you dealing with in New York?" Deegan said.

I shook my head.

Deegan grinned. "Sure," he said. "Of course you won't say. You don't give a fucking inch on anything."

"You're not dead," I said.

Deegan raised his eyebrows. Then he walked to my desk and poured another shot for himself.

"You get it together in New York, names, promises, the works, in detail and then we'll talk again."

"Where do I reach you?" I said.

Deegan paused, thought about that for a moment, then shrugged.

"I'll be with Madelaine," he said.

"I'll be in touch," I said.

Deegan picked up the whiskey glass and tossed the rest of the scotch down. He put the glass on my desk again and turned and walked to my door. He tugged his collar up higher.

"Raining like a bastard," he said, and went out.

THIRTY-FOUR

I spent the next day on the phone. I talked three or four times to Maguire in Brooklyn, and then twice to a guy from the New York Federal Attorney's office, a guy named Jennerette.

"Why don't you nail him for the gambling thing up there?" Jennerette said, "if it's so air tight."

"Because I'm trying to protect the player," I said.

"So why not let Deegan walk. He keeps quiet, you keep quiet?"

"Couple of reasons," I said. I'd already gone through them with Maguire and with the commander of the Brooklyn robbery squad. "He's walking around loose, with only the player to finger him, he might find it more sensible to ace the player. Also another kid died in this deal, kid named Danny Davis. I figure somebody has to pay dues for that."

243

"What's this kid Davis to you?" Jennerette said.

"Nothing," I said. "But somebody owes something for him; and I don't want the other kid to see Deegan walk away from this looking like a stand up guy."

"Witness protection isn't like doing time," Jennerette said.

"That's not it," I said. "I want my kid to see Deegan rat on his buddies."

There was silence on the phone.

"You want us to help you cover up a crime, so you can give some kid an object lesson?"

"You bet," I said.

Again silence on the phone.

"Why not try to get Deegan on the murder of this kid Davis?" Jennerette said.

"Expose my client," I said. "I'm trying to save this kid. He's got a future if I can save him."

"Mr. Fucking Rogers," Jennerette said.

"You get several guys that are better off the streets. Brooklyn cleans up a robbery that's been making them look bad. Witness Protection gets the chance to hang out with Bobby Deegan, always a treat. Who knows what you may find out once you get Deegan talking. Guy's a connected guy. You could end up on 'Nightline.' "

"Boss will end up on 'Nightline,' " Jennerette said. "Hold on a minute."

I could hear the phone being put down on the desk and the faint sounds of office noise: voices, other phones ringing, the tap, occasionally, of high-heeled shoes. There was maybe five minutes of this and then Jennerette came back on the phone.

"Okay," he said. "Deegan turns, and gives us the OTB job, we'll give him immunity and protection. If," Jennerette paused for the 'if' to sink in, "he delivers quality."

"But of course," I said.

"We'll be the judge of what's quality," he said.

"The rest of the crew in the OTB robbery," I said. "Is that quality?"

"Yes," Jennerette said.

"I'll get back to you," I said.

We hung up.

I went down to the alley back of my building and got my car and headed for Newton. It was nearly four in the afternoon and traffic was beginning to clog things. Boston was never meant for automobiles. The streets wound in the downtown section like cattle trails without any reasonable pattern and even in Back Bay, where the grid system had been applied when the old bay was filled in in the nineteenth century, the scale was too limited for automobiles in large number. In New York they drove faster, but for simple difficulty in getting from one part of town to another, Boston was, on a scale of ten, ten.

Storrow Drive would be standing still at this time. And so would the Mass. Pike. Shrewdly, I stayed off both and went straight out Commonwealth. So did everyone else. I hit every red light, and got to Newton at five thirty-five. Bobby and Madelaine were having cocktails. There was a pitcher of martinis on the coffee table. No one offered me one.

"Brooklyn will go for it," I told Deegan. He was sitting in a Barcalounger wearing a white cotton sweater over a crimson polo shirt, collar up. His acid-washed jeans were carefully ironed and his Top-Siders were new. "You turn on the OTB thing and they give you immunity and protection."

"And you?" he said. Madelaine sat on the foot of the Barcalounger, near his ankles, her left hand resting on his knee, sipping a martini from a thick lowball glass. She had her shoes off but otherwise looked as if she'd just come from work in a gray wrap-around dress.

"Me? You don't mention Dwayne, and he and I don't mention you," I said. "Nobody ever fixed a Taft game."

"What happens about Davis?"

"I got no control over that," I said. "But if there's no gambling case, I don't know how they'll make you for Davis."

"Danny Davis?" Madelaine said.

Deegan made a shushing motion with his hand.

"What about Danny?" Madelaine said. "Bobby, did you . . . "

"Put a lid on it, Madelaine. How do you know this guy hasn't got a wire?"

Madelaine looked as if she'd bitten into a sawdust donut. Her mouth shut and stayed shut.

"He's not going down for it," I said, "but Bobby had Danny Davis killed. Tried to have Dwayne killed. If he were going down for it you'd probably be an accessory to murder."

"I never . . . " she said, and that's as far as she got. Deegan leaned forward and grabbed her arm and yanked her over, so that she was sprawled on top of him on the lounger. With his face against hers, and his lips actually touching her lips, he said, "Shut up, you understand that? Shut your fucking trap."

I could see by the whiteness of his knuckles that he was squeezing her arm hard. She squirmed, pulling at his fingers.

"You understand?" he said again in a hoarse voice, holding her head in place with his left hand.

"Yes," she whispered, and he let her go. She got up abruptly and went and stood near the fireplace rubbing her arm where he'd squeezed it.

"You say what you want," Deegan said to me calmly. "I'm not saying anything at all about any murder stuff, that's not part of this deal. I had nothing to do with any murders."

"I'm not wired, Bobby," I said. "And I just wanted Madelaine to know who she was sleeping with. But for the record the deal doesn't include any murders."

"Fine," Deegan said. "Who do I talk to?"

"I'll set it up," I said. "You'll be here?"

"Right here," Deegan said.

THIRTY-FIVE

The next morning Dwayne bolted. He went into a washroom at the Lancaster Tap, opened the pebble glass window and went out and down the alley, leaving two campus cops having cheeseburgers and coffee and wondering what took Dwayne so long.

Chantel met him at the foot of the alley and they were off in the Trans Am, with Hawk behind them. He followed them to a house off Blue Hill Ave. near Mattapan Square. Watched them for a while until they settled in, and then he came and told me about it.

"You stuck with Chantel," I said. "You knew he wouldn't go without her."

Hawk nodded. "Dwayne can't drive," he said.

"He could have taken a cab," I said.

"Sure," Hawk said.

"Let's go see him," I said.

"Might make him run again," Hawk said. "I'm getting sick of chasing him."

"We need to talk," I said.

We went in Hawk's car. Out the expressway and onto Columbia Road toward Mattapan Square. Hawk was listening to an album by Kinky Friedman and the Texas Jewboys.

"What happened to Hugh Masekela?" I said.

"Next tape," Hawk said.

Hawk turned the Jag down Blue Hill Ave. and in another ten minutes we were pulling up in front of a three decker like a thousand others in Boston. Porches on the front of each floor with wooden railings. Shingle siding. Flat roof. The small yard out front was neatly trimmed. There were flowers in flower boxes on each floor. The house had been painted recently.

Hawk and I got out of the car. Everyone I saw was black, children mostly, and some older people. No one paid me any attention.

"First floor," Hawk said as we went up the steps to the porch. We went into the little entryway. The stairs went up the left side of the hall. There was a door in the right wall. I knocked. There were footsteps, and the door opened as far as the security chain inside would let it. A black woman looked out at us.

I said, "Hello, my name is Spenser, I'm

here to see Dwayne."

"No Dwayne here," she said.

"Yes there is, Ma'am," Hawk said. "I know he's here. Trans Am parked in the garage."

"Ask Chantel," I said. "They'll see me."

The door closed. Hawk stepped back out onto the porch and looked down the driveway. After a minute or two the footsteps returned and the door opened. This time it was Chantel. She looked out at me. Hawk came back from the porch.

"Wait a minute," Chantel said.

She closed the door. The chain bolt slid off, and then the door opened. Chantel stepped back. We went into a den with a television, a braided rug on the floor, a daybed covered with a paisley throw, and a big leather armchair. Beyond the den was a big old kitchen, the kind that families would spend most of their time in. Chantel led us through the den and into the kitchen. There was a big square table against the wall opposite the big gas stove. There was another daybed in the kitchen, this one built in with a headboard of the same upright pine boards that formed the wainscot. At the foot of the daybed was a big old black leather rocking chair. The linoleum floor was covered with another braided rug. A door off the kitchen led to what appeared to be a dining room, another opened on a bedroom. At the far end of the kitchen was a bathroom and pantry. An old, portly black man stood at an easel in the middle of the kitchen floor under a bright fluorescent light, painting a landscape in oils. The woman who had opened the door sat at the oilcloth-covered table with Dwayne. There was coffee and the remains of a pumpkin pie on the table.

Dwayne looked up at me as Chantel brought us in.

"What you want?" he said.

Chantel went over and sat beside him. She had on a white shirt and jeans and low black boots. A scarlet scarf was knotted at her throat. Hawk went and leaned on the door jamb as he had at Madelaine's. There was no one could lean on a door like Hawk. When he was still he was entirely still. There was no real evidence he was alive when he leaned on the door jamb. You couldn't even see him breathe.

There was an empty chair at the table so I pulled it out and sat. The old guy at the easel ignored me. He had on a blue bib apron with paint stains on it, and he had a cigar clenched in his teeth. His brush moved in confident dabbing motions on the canvas.

"I think I got this thing fixed," I said to Dwayne.

Dwayne stared at me without comment.

252

The woman got up and started to clear the table. She had on a yellow dress belted at the waist.

"Deegan was involved in a robbery in New York," I said. "To avoid prosecution on this gambling thing, he's going to testify against his associates in the robbery."

"So what's that mean for us?" Chantel said.

"Means you're clean. You can play basketball and sign with the Knicks for more than Ewing got — if the Clippers don't draft you — and live happily ever after."

"What about Bobby?" Dwayne said.

"After Bobby rats on his friends," I said, "he'll be in a witness protection program. New name, new place, new career. He won't have any chance, or any reason, to bother you," I said.

"How you get him to do that?" Dwayne said.

"Told him you'd testify against him on the gambling."

Dwayne stared at me. "I'd never squeal on nobody, man."

"He'd have killed you if we let him," I said.

"Don't matter about him," Dwayne said. "Matters 'bout me."

"You won't be a squealer even if the guy deserves to be squealed on," I said.

Dwayne thought about that for a minute,

then nodded slowly.

"Man's what he is, not what other people are," he said.

"Sure," I said. "But you won't have to testify, so long as Bobby thinks you will."

"Ought to know I wouldn't," Dwayne said. "Dwayne Woodcock don't do no squealing."

"Fortunately, Bobby Deegan does," I said.

"Don't believe Bobby'll do that," Dwayne said.

"Did you believe he'd have somebody try to kill you?" I said.

"Don't have to be Bobby," Dwayne said.

Chantel made an angry little *tsh* sound, and Dwayne glanced at her. He didn't speak. But after he'd looked at Chantel for a moment he began to barely nod his head.

"Who else know we here?" Dwayne said.

"Just Hawk and me," I said.

"You going to tell?" Dwayne said.

"No," I said. "But you don't need to hide. Deegan's going to be wrapped up. You can play ball."

Dwayne shook his head.

"We going to stay here for a while," he said. "See what happens. See if it's like you say."

"Coach Dunham will want to talk," I said.

"Things be like you say," Dwayne said, "I call him in a while."

"There's another piece of the deal," I said. Dwayne waited.

"You learn to read," I said.

"Nobody tell Dwayne Woodcock what he do and don't do."

I nodded my head at Hawk. "Man saved your life a while ago," I said.

Dwayne looked over at Hawk and nodded his head sharply once.

"You owe him," I said.

"Can't read," Hawk said, "you gonna be a dumb fuck all your life, excuse me, Chantel, and whitey gonna yank you around."

"He's right," Chantel said in a flat voice.

"Nobody call Dwayne Woodcock a dumb fuck," Dwayne said. He started to get up.

"Sit down, Dwayne," Hawk said. "We went to all this trouble to save your ass, I don't want to have to shoot you now."

Dwayne was on his feet staring at Hawk. Hawk remained as still on the door jamb as he had. The old guy kept painting. For all he cared we could have been on television.

Chantel said, "Dwayne, the man saved your life and mine. You know you got to learn to read. Both of them saved your life."

Dwayne stood for a long moment without speaking, then he sat back down.

"College will be able to arrange for a reading specialist," I said. "Coach Dunham can get that going."

Dwayne nodded.

"I want your word on it," I said.

Dwayne stared at me. I waited. Chantel banged her elbow into his upper arm.

"Dwayne," she said, making it two long syllables.

Dwayne still stared. Then he said, "You got it."

"Thank you," I said.

I looked at the painting the old guy was working on. It was mountains with a valley and a lake in the valley.

"White Mountains," he said. "New Hampshire."

"Un huh," I said and headed for the door. In the Jaguar, driving back up Blue Hill Ave. Hawk said, "Grateful motherfucker."

"Maybe he is," I said, "but can't show it."

"Or maybe he ain't," Hawk said.

THIRTY-SIX

Susan and I were having dinner at a place called Rarities in the Charles Hotel in Cambridge.

Outside the bank of picture windows Charles Square was beginning to look autumnal, and the first pumpkins and cornstalks were clustered around the display base of the Charles Square sign. Harvard students were back; parents, visiting, were lounging around the hotel lobby looking a little startled that they had kids in college.

"They convicted Deegan's friends today," I said.

She was reading the menu closely, peering through the crimson-rimmed twelve-dollar half glasses that she bought in Neiman Marcus.

"Bobby Deegan? Dwayne Woodcock's friend?" she said.

"Yeah, Bobby sang them all right into the

state penal institution at Ossining."

"And Bobby?"

"Disappeared into the witness protection program."

"Do those work?" Susan said.

"They work if the guys after you have limited resources, and they work if the guy in the program isn't a dope. But most of them are dopes. They can't stay away from it. They knock over a crap game or they show up in Vegas on a gambling junket and someone recognizes them, or they get in a fight and someone hears about them."

"Do you think it will for Bobby Deegan?"

The waiter came solicitously by and took our order.

"Deegan's smart," I said, "but he's been a wiseguy his whole life. He's never held a job, except being a crook. They'll set him up with new identity, papers, some money, a house. And they'll place him in a job. Selling real estate, say, or being a short order cook; that kind of thing. And he'll go to work every day and after a while his boss will tell him to do something and Bobby won't want to and they'll come to words and Bobby will pop him on the nose and quit and pretty soon he's back into being a crook, and after a while somebody will recognize him, or he'll get busted, or whatever. If it's the mob after you, then you're in trouble, because they've got time and money and connections and no passion. Killing you is a wise management decision for them. Passion cools, except you and me, Hotpants, but wise business decisions by the mob are forever. His friends may forget about who put them away, or they may not."

The waiter brought Susan some sweetbreads with grilled fruit. For me he brought oysters.

"Hotpants?" Susan said.

"Yeah, that's why the oysters," I said.

Susan ate a very small bite of sweetbread.

"How is Dwayne?" she said.

"Fine," I said. "Surly, arrogant, uncommunicative, and the holder of a two-point-five-million contract over three years."

"Is Chantel with him?"

"Yes," I said.

"Good," Susan said. "Can he read?"

"Some," I said. "Chantel says he got to about third grade level over the summer."

"That's very good progress," Susan said. "It's only been, what, five months?"

"Yes."

I slurped an oyster and gestured with my wine list at the waiter.

"Gewürztraminer," I said. "The Trimbach."

He smiled approvingly and hustled off after the wine. Waiters smile approvingly if you order cough syrup. I finished my oysters. The waiter served the wine. Susan finished her sweetbreads. We each took a sip of wine. Around us the soft sound of conversation, the gentle noise of steaks being cut and soup being spooned. The light was soft and the encroaching September evening darkened the view through the windows.

"You can't stand Dwayne, can you?" Susan said.

"No," I said, "who could? Even Hawk doesn't like him and Hawk doesn't have feelings about anybody."

"Except you," Susan said.

"And you," I said.

"Chantel loves him," Susan said.

"Love's different," I said. "It doesn't alter 'where it alteration finds.' "

"I know," Susan said.

The waiter appeared with barbecued duck for Susan, venison for me.

"And yet you just stuck at it and wouldn't let Dwayne destroy himself even though they tried to kill you, and it was hard, and there was no reason to care about him."

"You think I shouldn't have?" I said.

"No, I think you should have. But, God, he's obnoxious."

"You have obnoxious patients," I said.

Susan smiled. "I'll say," she said.

"Dwayne is one of the best that ever lived at what he does," I said.

"Which is playing basketball," Susan said.

"Yes. Not brain surgery, but something."

"And?" Susan said.

"And I like Chantel," I said.

Susan smiled, and her smile widened as she looked at me. Then she picked up her wine glass and raised it toward me a little and held it for a moment.

"Is this a good omen?" I said.

"If I were you," she said, "I'd have more oysters."

THORNDIKE-MAGNA hopes you have enjoyed this Large Print book. All our Large Print titles are designed for easy reading, and all our books are made to last. Other Thorndike Press or Magna Print books are available at your library, through selected bookstores, or directly from the publishers. For more information about current and upcoming titles, please call or mail your name and address to:

THORNDIKE PRESS
P.O. Box 159
Thorndike, Maine 04986
(800) 223-6121
(207) 948-2962 (in Maine and Canada call collect)

or in the United Kingdom:

MAGNA PRINT BOOKS
Long Preston, Near Skipton
North Yorkshire,
England BD23 4ND
(07294) 225

There is no obligation, of course.